倍斯特出版事業有限公司
Best Publishing Ltd.

U0077391

雅思口說聖經

Amanda Chou ◎ 著

英式發音
MP3

提供六種性格相異的答法
以此演練官方必考主題 秒成百變答題高手

精煉必考主題，狂「偷時間」

從官方試題中精選**核心必考**主題並附音檔，汰除過舊且不合時宜的話題，以最省時方式講出**具體**和**豐富**的回答，巧取雅思口說8.0以上的高分。

數百句單句口譯練習，答題思路瞬間活化

演練各主題的單句口譯，大幅提升英文思考和答題反應力，在**抽象類**和**個人感受**的主題上亦能游刃有餘獲取考官青睞。

Author
作者序

根據一項統計，雅思口說考到 7 分以上的考生只佔了非常低的比例，對許多雅思聽力和閱讀都考到 8-9 分，但是在寫作和口說單項經過數次報考仍停在 6-6.5 的考生來說，備考期間除了所衍生的挫折感外，更會在報考後有著疑惑感。對於整場口試英語都滔滔不絕地講，但只勉為其難地考取 6 分的考生，主要原因則是在語法、表達是否道地和是否切中問題核心回答。（這部分可以經由這本書而大幅改進）在釐清幾項原因後，對於要考取 6.5 分的考生來說，一定要掌握的原則是要講完話題卡題，這部分就需要反應能力。考生可能會突然在話題卡題遇到自己不會說的題目，而淪為只能跟考官乾瞪眼的份。這也是很多考生討厭話題卡題的原因。對於想要以最省時的時間一次就考取口說高分的考生來說，主要要注意的是掌握核心且反覆出現的話題，並經由不斷地演練漸進式融合成自己的回答。這也是這本書撰寫的主要原因，幫助考生篩選和汰除掉某些話題，將時間真正花在刀口上，演練會考的真題。

在這本書中，選取了以**《劍橋雅思系列》**當中的劍橋雅思

9-15 的主題（在目次和書籍中以《劍 9》簡稱並加上 TP，T 指的是 Test，而 P 指的是 Part）和**《劍橋雅思官方指南》**當中重複出現、完全一樣或近似的主題，考生在備考上可以更無往不利。在規劃上要選取這樣類別的主題又要進行分類，確實有一定的難度在，但最終還是能從雅思官方試題等找出蛛絲馬跡，並歸納和破解雅思口說的出題脈絡，在雅思口說的備考上，若用對方法，比起雅思聽力和閱讀更好攻略（雖然對大多數考生來說，聽力和閱讀單項更好準備），口說話題不像聽力和閱讀有更龐大的題庫和主題等等的，要在口說中遇到相似或近似的主題是輕而易舉。口說必考話題最終可以歸納出這幾類，幾乎全離不開**食、衣、住、行、育、樂**的主題，所以只要掌握這個大原則並經由書中精選的話題系統化的練習就能迅速攻略雅思口說，且成效顯著，絕對比寫一堆聽力和閱讀試題達到的成效更事半功倍。在這當中，口說常重複出現的考題（儘管是經由改寫過的試題，還是換湯不換藥，重新組織下就能應答），包含了音樂、運動、旅行、交通工具、購物和餐廳等，在劍橋雅思的歷屆試題和實際考試中不斷地重複出現，所以務必要演練所有話題後才報考。

而除了在 part 1 到 part 3 的循環必考主題外，另外加入了 Part 4 的最後衝刺 61 題試題，考生甚至能從目次和回答內容中看出，這些話題還與最新的劍橋雅思 15 的話題有所重疊，所以絕對是備考利器，讓考生能舉一反三。另外要說明的是，其他在目次中沒註明標示的，像是顏色類等的話題，在其他本劍橋雅思或是實際考試中仍有出現，只是這本書的標示和規劃是以考生備考心理為主來規劃（因為考生大多都準備近幾年的考試話題）沒有標示到的話題被選進書籍中代表仍有其重要性在。另外是關於思考的部分，考生不用把某些話題想的太過單一，例如釣魚的興趣（這跟雅思口説有關嘛!?），但這個回答就適用於實際考試中的話題卡題中突然被問到你有什麼嗜好，而你在準備的時候想不到要如何回答卻因為看過書中的答案而能迅速發揮效果，出其不意地答好很多題。甚至當中的某些敘述又能應用在其他話題中，例如和上司的互動，就又可以以約上司去釣魚或在面試話題中，其實面試官已經很滿意了，只是在了解你平常生活在做些什麼，又能以釣魚話題發揮在其他雅思口説或工作面試中的主題。口説的回答和搭配上是可以很靈活且趣味橫生的，千萬不要小看每個回答和主題。一些看似無關的主題，例如洞穴的回答，又能用在觀光和特別體驗的話題卡題中。所以這本書是很巧妙靈活的一本，能迅速拓展答題思路，在考試中不跟別人的回答撞車。這點是至關重要的，你要表現出你自己。許多考生都千篇一律地答國內的節慶時，你卻能答書中其他國外的節慶，就迅速脱穎而出獲取更高分數。最後相信所有考生只要持之以恆的練習最終都能一戰而勝獲取理想成績。

Amanda Chou

使用說明

INSTRUCTIONS

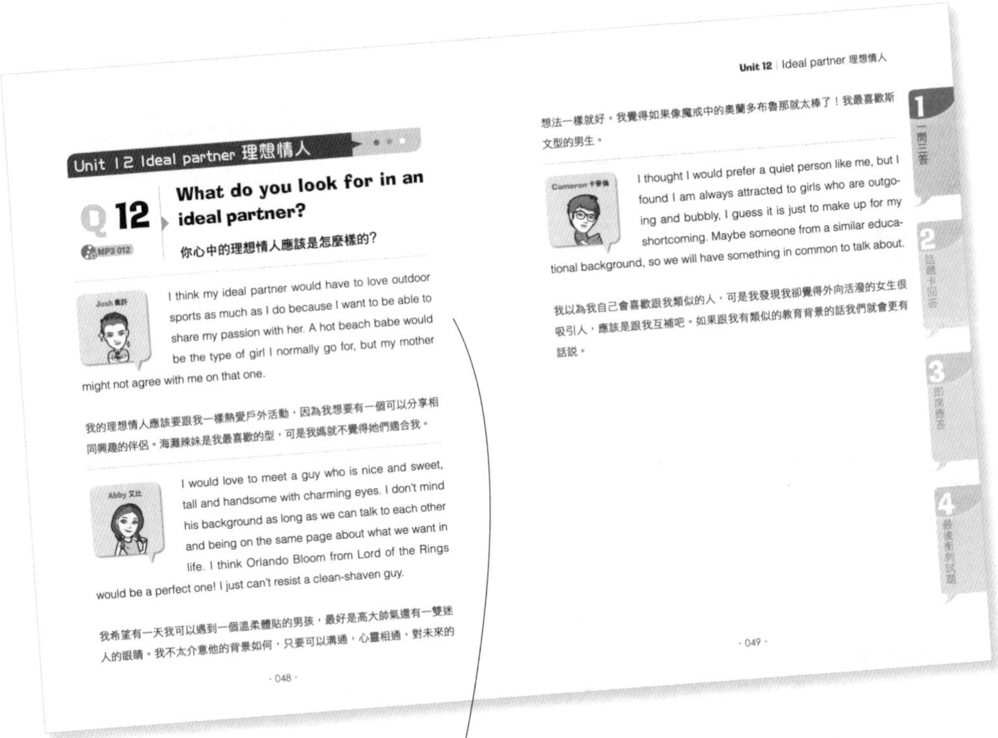

Unit 12 Ideal partner 理想情人

Q 12 What do you look for in an ideal partner?

你心中的理想情人應該是怎麼樣的？

MP3 012

Josh 喬許

I think my ideal partner would have to love outdoor sports as much as I do because I want to be able to share my passion with her. A hot beach babe would be the type of girl I normally go for, but my mother might not agree with me on that one.

我的理想情人應該要跟我一樣熱愛戶外活動，因為我想要有一個可以分享相同興趣的伴侶。海灘辣妹是我最喜歡的型，可是我媽就不覺得她們適合我。

Abby 艾比

I would love to meet a guy who is nice and sweet, tall and handsome with charming eyes. I don't mind his background as long as we can talk to each other and being on the same page about what we want in life. I think Orlando Bloom from Lord of the Rings would be a perfect one! I just can't resist a clean-shaven guy.

我希望有一天我可以遇到一個溫柔體貼的男孩，最好是高大帥氣還有一雙迷人的眼睛。我不太介意他的背景如何，只要可以溝通，心靈相通，對未來的想法一樣就好。我覺得如果像魔戒中的奧蘭多布魯那就太棒了！我最喜歡斯文型的男生。

Cameron 卡麥倫

I thought I would prefer a quiet person like me, but I found I am always attracted to girls who are outgoing and bubbly, I guess it is just to make up for my shortcoming. Maybe someone from a similar educational background, so we will have something in common to talk about.

我以為我自己會喜歡跟我類似的人，可是我發現我卻覺得外向活潑的女生很吸引人，應該是跟我互補吧。如果跟我有類似的教育背景的話我們就會更有話說。

1 一問三答

2 話題卡回答

3 即席應答

4 最後衝刺試題

Part 1 好的開始就是成功的一半：

· 規劃一問三答神效拓展答題思路，並收錄百句道地用語，穩守基礎類核心話題，漸入佳境地迎戰話題卡題。

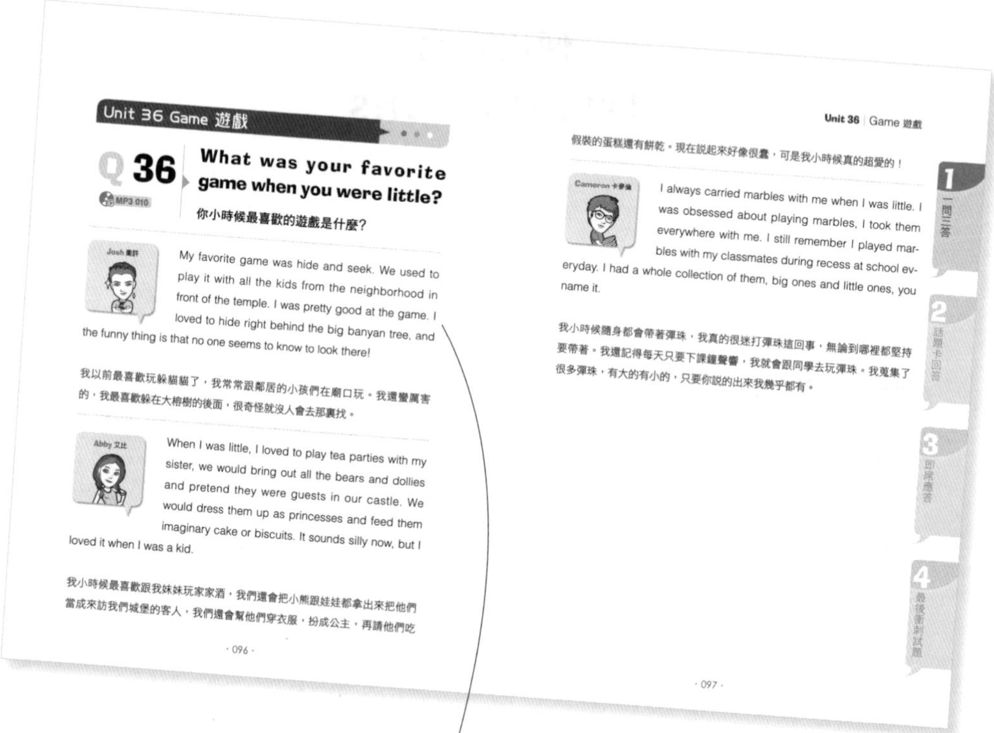

Unit 36 Game 遊戲

Q 36 What was your favorite game when you were little?

MP3 010

你小時候最喜歡的遊戲是什麼？

Josh 喬許

My favorite game was hide and seek. We used to play it with all the kids from the neighborhood in front of the temple. I was pretty good at the game. I loved to hide right behind the big banyan tree, and the funny thing is that no one seems to know to look there!

我以前最喜歡玩躲貓貓了，我常常跟鄰居的小孩們在廟口玩。我還蠻厲害的，我最喜歡躲在大榕樹的後面，很奇怪就沒人會去那裏找。

Abby 艾比

When I was little, I loved to play tea parties with my sister, we would bring out all the bears and dollies and pretend they were guests in our castle. We would dress them up as princesses and feed them imaginary cake or biscuits. It sounds silly now, but I loved it when I was a kid.

我小時候最喜歡跟我妹妹玩家家酒，我們還會把小熊跟娃娃都拿出來把他們當成來訪我們城堡的客人，我們還會幫他們穿衣服，扮成公主，再請他們吃假裝的蛋糕還有餅乾。現在說起來好像很蠢，可是我小時候真的超愛的！

Cameron 卡麥倫

I always carried marbles with me when I was little. I was obsessed about playing marbles, I took them everywhere with me. I still remember I played marbles with my classmates during recess at school everyday. I had a whole collection of them, big ones and little ones, you name it.

我小時候隨身都會帶著彈珠，我真的很迷打彈珠這回事，無論到哪裡都堅持要帶著。我還記得每天只要下課鐘聲響，我就會跟同學去玩彈珠。我蒐集了很多彈珠，有大的有小的，只要你說的出來我幾乎都有。

海量練習：

· 近 100 題一問三答規劃，大幅改善考生內容重複性過高且失去個人特色的回答，瞬間豐富化答題內容，立刻答出令考官青睞有加的回答。

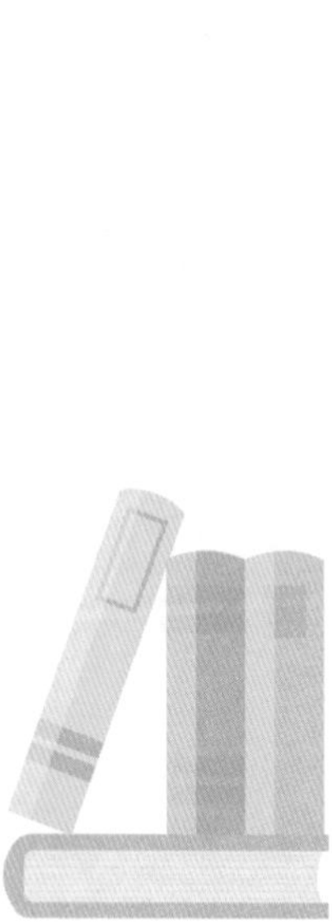

Part 2 佔盡先機：

- 事先演練無敵話題，備考即練就「隨機應變」猛實力，以流利英語講完兩分鐘話題卡題，穩拿僅 15% 左右考生才考得到的 7.0 口説佳績。

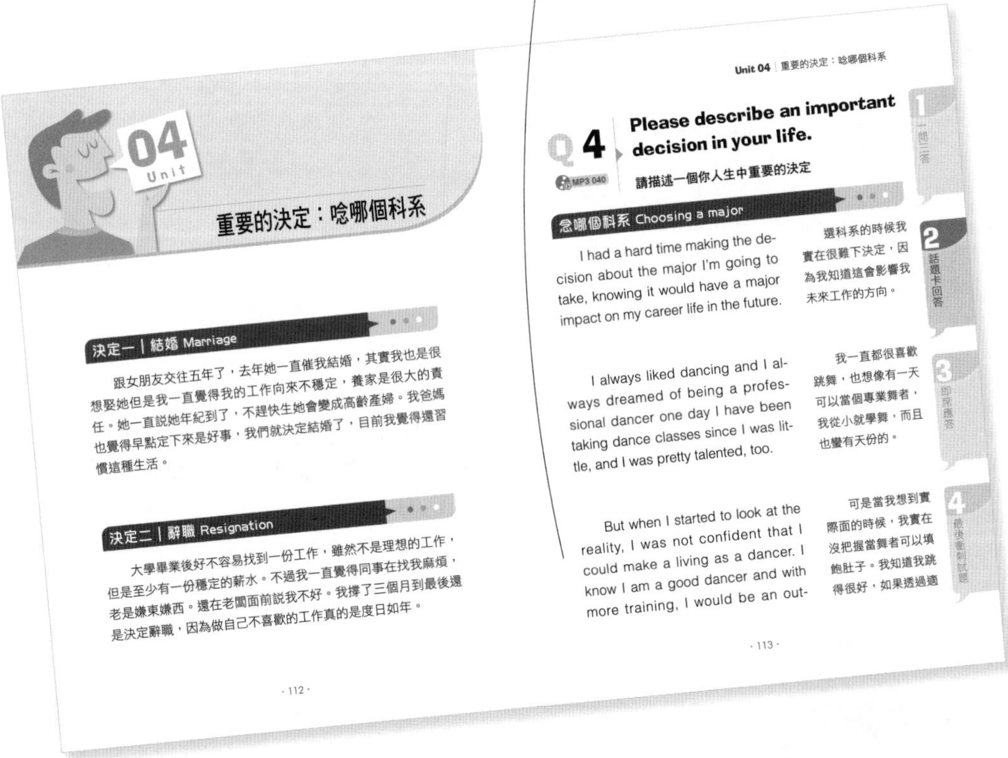

04 Unit

重要的決定：唸哪個科系

決定一｜結婚 Marriage

跟女朋友交往五年了，去年她一直催我結婚，其實我也是很想娶她但是我一直覺得我的工作向來不穩定，養家是很大的責任。她一直説她年紀到了，不趕快生她會變成高齡產婦。我爸媽也覺得早點定下來是好事，我們就決定結婚了，目前我覺得還習慣這種生活。

決定二｜辭職 Resignation

大學畢業後好不容易找到一份工作，雖然不是理想的工作，但是至少有一份穩定的薪水。不過我一直覺得同事在找我麻煩，老是嫌東嫌西。還在老闆面前説我不好。我撐了三個月到最後還是決定辭職，因為做自己不喜歡的工作真的是度日如年。

· 112 ·

Unit 04｜重要的決定：唸哪個科系

Q 4 Please describe an important decision in your life.

MP3 040

請描述一個你人生中重要的決定

唸哪個科系 Choosing a major

I had a hard time making the decision about the major I'm going to take, knowing it would have a major impact on my career life in the future.

選科系的時候我實在很難下決定，因為我知道這會影響我未來工作的方向。

I always liked dancing and I always dreamed of being a professional dancer one day I have been taking dance classes since I was little, and I was pretty talented, too.

我一直都很喜歡跳舞，也想像有一天可以當個專業舞者，我從小就學舞，而且也蠻有天份的。

But when I started to look at the reality, I was not confident that I could make a living as a dancer. I know I am a good dancer and with more training, I would be an out-

可是當我想到實際面的時候，我實在沒把握當舞者可以填飽肚子。我知道我跳得很好，如果透過適

1 一問三答

2 話題卡回答

3 即席應答

4 最後衝刺試題

· 113 ·

Unit 09 | 卡通/故事人物：海底總動員多莉

Dory is this blue fish with yellow fins, she suffers from short-term memory loss, but she never takes it as a problem! I guess her memory is just too short to remember it anyway!

多莉是一隻藍色帶有黃色鰭的魚，她常常只有短期失憶症，可是她從來不覺得這是個問題。我想也是，因為她根本記不得她有記憶的問題！

Most people would think she is just a forgetful and careless fish. But I see her differently. I think she is the eternal optimist, she is always so happy and excited about things.

大部分的人會覺得她是一隻健忘又粗心的魚。可是我不這麼想，我倒覺得她是終極的樂觀者！她對每件事總是那麼的正面，積極的去面對。

Her level of excitement is like she experiences things for the first time. I guess she is, because she can't remember she has done it before. Same as the frustration and disappointments, she doesn't hold

她對每件事的興奮程度就好像她從來沒做過這回事，我想也是，因為她不記得她有做過。同樣的，不高興或是失望的事

· 134 ·

things against anyone because she can't remember what they have said or done to her any way. I guess it is probably not a bad thing to forget things that bother you after all.

她也忘得快，她對人沒有敵意，因為她早忘了別人是怎麼對她。我覺得忘記不好的事其實是件好事。

There is a sequel coming out about finding Dory this time. I am looking forward to seeing what happens after they found Nemo and how she got lost. I am sure it will be a great story!

海底總動員的續集要上映了，這次是有關尋找多莉的事。我很期待想知道他們找到尼莫之後多莉是怎樣不見的，這故事一定會很有趣。

· 135 ·

1 一問三答

2 話題卡回答

3 即席應答

4 最後衝刺試題

「中譯英」答題強化：

· 以口説話題演練「中譯英」並反覆練習所有話題直至養成答題反射動作，整場考試均流利應答，降低因為緊張或對考題不確定感的影響。

Part 3 如虎添翼：

· 練習即席應答必考話題，在抽象類話題的應答中均能從容不迫、言之有物，輕而易舉獲取 7.5-8.0 等更高佳績。

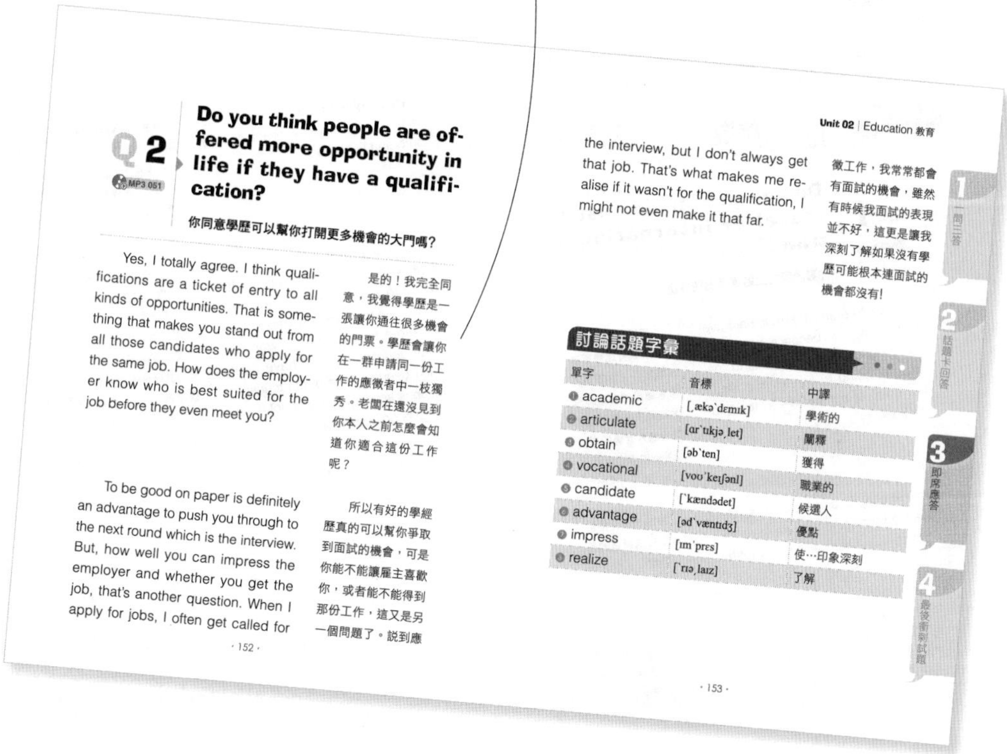

Unit 02 | Education 教育

Q2 Do you think people are offered more opportunity in life if they have a qualification?

MP3 051

你同意學歷可以幫你打開更多機會的大門嗎？

Yes, I totally agree. I think qualifications are a ticket of entry to all kinds of opportunities. That is something that makes you stand out from all those candidates who apply for the same job. How does the employer know who is best suited for the job before they even meet you?

是的！我完全同意，我覺得學歷是一張讓你通往很多機會的門票。學歷會讓你在一群申請同一份工作的應徵者中一枝獨秀。老闆在還沒見到你本人之前怎麼會知道你適合這份工作呢？

To be good on paper is definitely an advantage to push you through to the next round which is the interview. But, how well you can impress the employer and whether you get the job, that's another question. When I apply for jobs, I often get called for the interview, but I don't always get that job. That's what makes me realise if it wasn't for the qualification, I might not even make it that far.

所以有好的學經歷真的可以幫你爭取到面試的機會，可是你能不能讓雇主喜歡你，或者能不能得到那份工作，這又是另一個問題了。說到應徵工作，我常常都會有面試的機會，雖然有時候我面試的表現並不好，這更是讓我深刻了解如果沒有學歷可能根本連面試的機會都沒有！

討論話題字彙

單字	音標	中譯
❶ academic	[ˌækəˋdɛmɪk]	學術的
❷ articulate	[ɑrˋtɪkjəˌlet]	闡釋
❸ obtain	[əbˋten]	獲得
❹ vocational	[voʊˋkeɪʃənl]	職業的
❺ candidate	[ˋkændədet]	候選人
❻ advantage	[ədˋvæntɪdʒ]	優點
❼ impress	[ɪmˋprɛs]	使…印象深刻
❽ realize	[ˋrɪəˌlaɪz]	了解

1 一問三答　2 話題卡回答　3 即席應答　4 最後衝刺試題

· 152 ·　· 153 ·

即學即用＋瞬間進步「1-2.5」分：

· 正中必考話題核心並輔以高分答案，面對五花八門的考題總能釐清思路，迅速組織出高分回答。

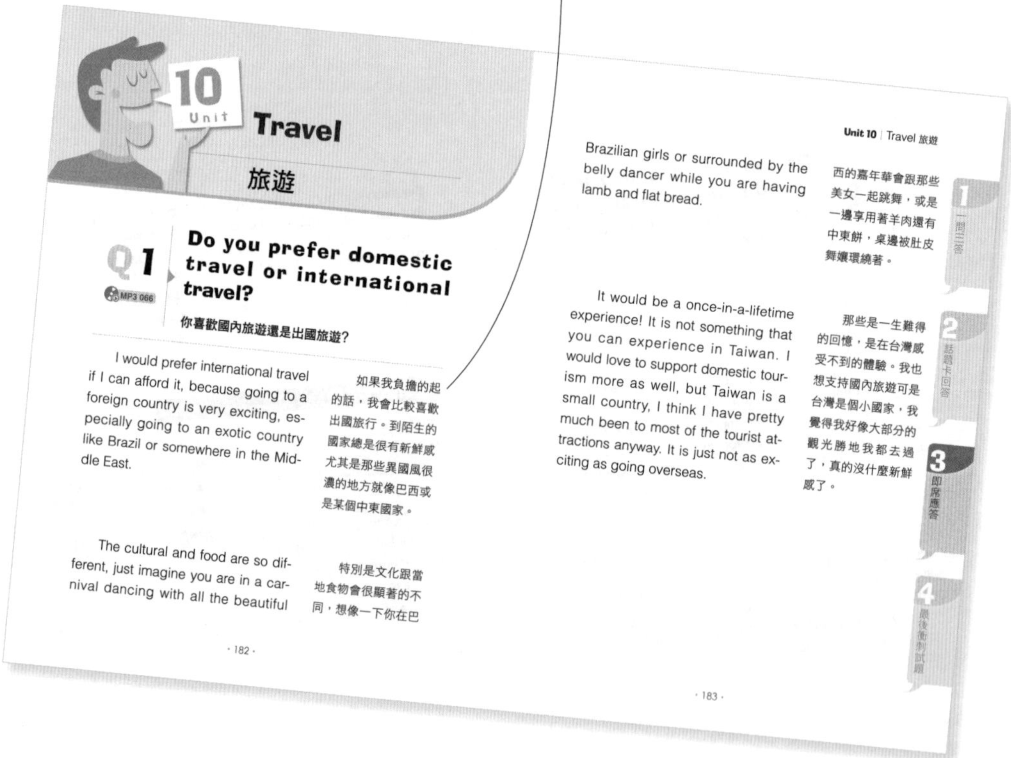

10 Unit

Travel

旅遊

Q1 MP3 066

Do you prefer domestic travel or international travel?

你喜歡國內旅遊還是出國旅遊？

I would prefer international travel if I can afford it, because going to a foreign country is very exciting, especially going to an exotic country like Brazil or somewhere in the Middle East.

如果我負擔的起的話，我會比較喜歡出國旅行。到陌生的國家總是很有新鮮感尤其是那些異國風很濃的地方就像巴西或是某個中東國家。

The cultural and food are so different, just imagine you are in a carnival dancing with all the beautiful

特別是文化跟當地食物會很顯著的不同，想像一下你在巴

· 182 ·

Unit 10 | Travel 旅遊

Brazilian girls or surrounded by the belly dancer while you are having lamb and flat bread.

西的嘉年華會跟那些美女一起跳舞，或是一邊享用著羊肉還有中東餅，桌邊被肚皮舞孃環繞著。

It would be a once-in-a-lifetime experience! It is not something that you can experience in Taiwan. I would love to support domestic tourism more as well, but Taiwan is a small country, I think I have pretty much been to most of the tourist attractions anyway. It is just not as exciting as going overseas.

那些是一生難得的回憶，是在台灣感受不到的體驗。我也想支持國內旅遊可是台灣是個小國家，我覺得我好像大部分的觀光勝地我都去過了，真的沒什麼新鮮感了。

1 一問三答
2 話題卡回答
3 即席應答
4 最後衝刺試題

· 183 ·

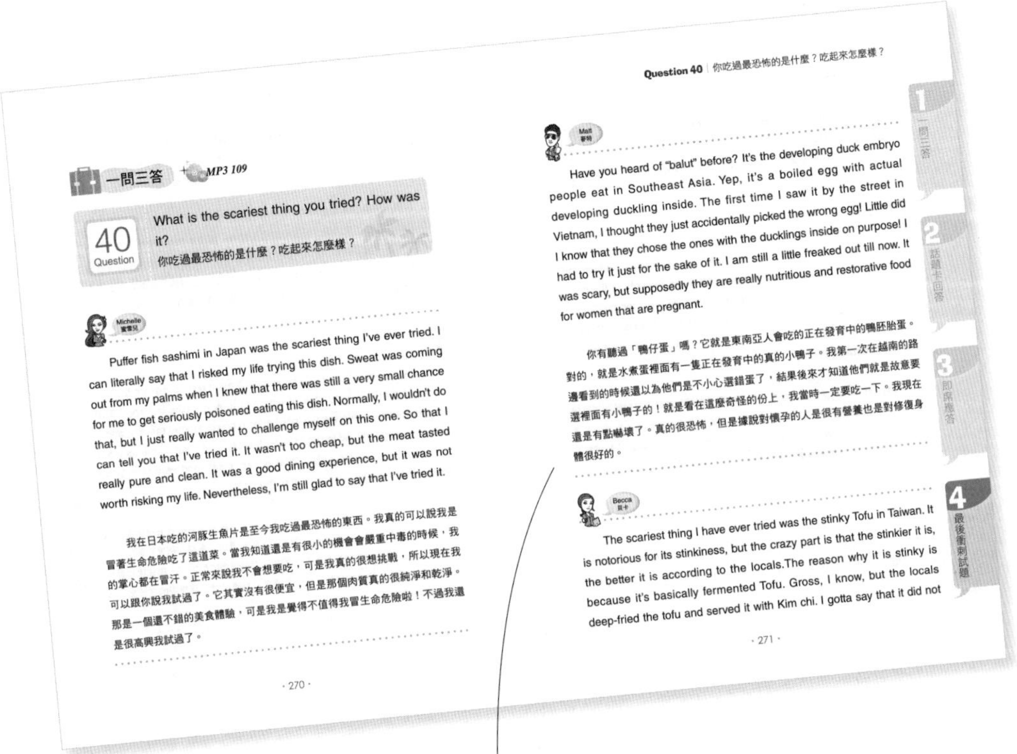

Question 40 你吃過最恐怖的是什麼？吃起來怎麼樣？

一問三答 MP3 109

40 Question

What is the scariest thing you tried? How was it?

你吃過最恐怖的是什麼？吃起來怎麼樣？

Michelle 蜜雪兒

Puffer fish sashimi in Japan was the scariest thing I've ever tried. I can literally say that I risked my life trying this dish. Sweat was coming out from my palms when I knew that there was still a very small chance for me to get seriously poisoned eating this dish. Normally, I wouldn't do that, but I just really wanted to challenge myself on this one. So that I can tell you that I've tried it. It wasn't too cheap, but the meat tasted really pure and clean. It was a good dining experience, but it was not worth risking my life. Nevertheless, I'm still glad to say that I've tried it.

我在日本吃的河豚生魚片是至今我吃過最恐怖的東西。我真的可以說我是冒著生命危險吃了這道菜。當我知道還是有很小的機會會嚴重中毒的時候，我的掌心都在冒汗。正常來說我不會想要吃，可是我真的很想挑戰，所以現在我可以跟你說我試過了。它其實沒有很便宜，但是那個肉質真的很純淨和乾淨。那是一個還不錯的美食體驗，可是我是覺得不值得我冒生命危險啦！不過我還是很高興我試過了。

· 270 ·

Matt 麥特

Have you heard of "balut" before? It's the developing duck embryo people eat in Southeast Asia. Yep, it's a boiled egg with actual developing duckling inside. The first time I saw it by the street in Vietnam, I thought they just accidentally picked the wrong egg! Little did I know that they chose the ones with the ducklings inside on purpose! I had to try it just for the sake of it. I am still a little freaked out till now. It was scary, but supposedly they are really nutritious and restorative food for women that are pregnant.

你有聽過「鴨仔蛋」嗎？它就是東南亞人會吃的正在發育中的鴨胚胎蛋。對的，就是水煮蛋裡面有一隻正在發育中的真的小鴨子。我第一次在越南的路邊看到的時候還以為他們是不小心選錯蛋了，結果後來才知道他們就是故意要選裡面有小鴨子的！就是看在這麼奇怪的份上，我當時一定要吃一下。我現在還是有點嚇壞了。真的很恐怖，但是據說對懷孕的人是很有營養也是對修復身體很好的。

Becca 貝卡

The scariest thing I have ever tried was the stinky Tofu in Taiwan. It is notorious for its stinkiness, but the crazy part is that the stinkier it is, the better it is according to the locals.The reason why it is stinky is because it's basically fermented Tofu. Gross, I know, but the locals deep-fried the tofu and served it with Kim chi. I gotta say that it did not

· 271 ·

1 一問三答

2 話題卡回答

3 即席應答

4 最後衝刺試題

Part 4 達於顛峰：

· 使用更具代表性的衝刺話題，額外強化應變能力和答題穩定性，大幅降低考試失常和運氣影響等因素，自信獲取高分。

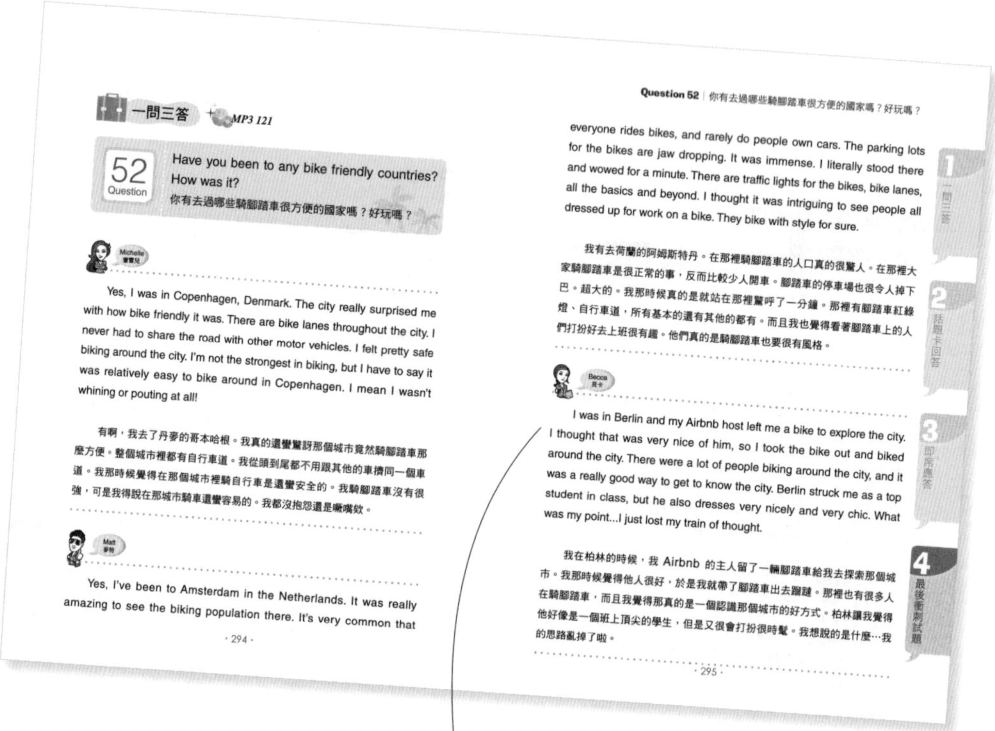

一問三答 MP3 121

52 Question
Have you been to any bike friendly countries? How was it?
你有去過哪些騎腳踏車很方便的國家嗎？好玩嗎？

Michelle 蜜雪兒

Yes, I was in Copenhagen, Denmark. The city really surprised me with how bike friendly it was. There are bike lanes throughout the city. I never had to share the road with other motor vehicles. I felt pretty safe biking around the city. I'm not the strongest in biking, but I have to say it was relatively easy to bike around in Copenhagen. I mean I wasn't whining or pouting at all!

有啊，我去了丹麥的哥本哈根。我真的還蠻驚訝那個城市竟然騎腳踏車那麼方便。整個城市裡都有自行車道。我從頭到尾都不用跟其他的車擠同一個車道。我那時候覺得在那個城市裡騎自行車是還蠻安全的。我騎腳踏車沒有很強，可是我得說在那城市騎車還蠻容易的。我都沒抱怨還是嘟嘴欸。

Matt 麥特

Yes, I've been to Amsterdam in the Netherlands. It was really amazing to see the biking population there. It's very common that everyone rides bikes, and rarely do people own cars. The parking lots for the bikes are jaw dropping. It was immense. I literally stood there and wowed for a minute. There are traffic lights for the bikes, bike lanes, all the basics and beyond. I thought it was intriguing to see people all dressed up for work on a bike. They bike with style for sure.

我有去荷蘭的阿姆斯特丹。在那裡騎腳踏車的人口真的很驚人。在那裡大家騎腳踏車是很正常的事，反而比較少人開車。腳踏車的停車場也很令人掉下巴。超大的。我那時候真的是就站在那裡驚呼了一分鐘。那裡有腳踏車紅綠燈、自行車道，所有基本的還有其他的都有。而且我也覺得看著腳踏車上的人們打扮好去上班很有趣。他們真的是騎腳踏車也要很有風格。

Becca 貝卡

I was in Berlin and my Airbnb host left me a bike to explore the city. I thought that was very nice of him, so I took the bike out and biked around the city. There were a lot of people biking around the city, and it was a really good way to get to know the city. Berlin struck me as a top student in class, but he also dresses very nicely and very chic. What was my point...I just lost my train of thought.

我在柏林的時候，我 Airbnb 的主人留了一輛腳踏車給我去探索那個城市。我那時候覺得他人很好，於是我就帶了腳踏車出去蹓躂。那裡也有很多人在騎腳踏車，而且我覺得那真的是一個認識那個城市的好方式。柏林讓我覺得他好像是一個班上頂尖的學生，但是又很會打扮很時髦。我想說的是什麼…我的思路亂掉了啦。

1 一問三答 2 話題卡回答 3 即席應答 4 最後衝刺試題

· 294 · · 295 ·

學習速度 5 倍強化：

· 將所有話題均內化，打通腦海英語表達的「任督二脈」，腦海中內建千句高分表達，越學進步越神速，只花費 1/5 的時間就考取其他考生的同等成績。

Contents 目次

Part 1 一問三答

Part 2 話題卡回答

Part 3 即席應答

Part 4 最後衝刺試題

・自然景觀：瀑布、湖泊、國家公園、大峽谷、美景、嗜好（健行等）

・新的事物和令人興奮的事 ——《劍9》T2P2

・觀光客參訪的地區等

——《劍官》T2P2/《劍官》T2P3

・描述故事 ——《劍官》T2P2

・游泳——《劍15》T3P1

・運動、水上運動、比賽等

·衣服、配備

·飲食、名產、食物和飲食習慣

·購物、購物中心、旅行時購物

‧運輸、交通工具、腳踏車、觀光旅行、住宿

Part 1

一問三答

· **真題重現：** 以劍橋雅思 9-15 和劍橋雅思官方指南話題為基準，用必考語庫來練習，事半功倍考取雅思口說高分。

· 與坊間雅思口說話題大有區別，以官方話題為依據，時間精確花在刀口上，最快速掌握口說考試話題並一次就獲取高分。

Unit 1 Hometown 家鄉

Q1 Can you tell me something about your hometown?

MP3 001

可以告訴有關你家鄉的一些事嗎？

Josh 喬許

During my upbringing, I was lucky enough to be raised in Heng Chuan, a small town at the southern end of Taiwan right by the famous beach area called Kenting. Like every other kid growing up in the area, I spent a lot of time under the sun doing surfing and snorkeling. You don't get that kind of lifestyle elsewhere!

我很幸運的我小時候在恆春長大，恆春是台灣南邊的一個小鎮，就在有名的墾丁海域旁邊。每個恆春長大的小孩從小就花很多時間在戶外衝浪和浮潛，我也不例外。別的地方可找不到這種生活方式呢！

Abby 艾比

I was born in Kaohsiung, the 2nd largest city located in southern Taiwan. I have always been a city girl, and I love the hustle and bustle, and Kaohsiung city offers exactly that. There are numbers of famous night markets adjacent to charming beaches nearby. Being a tropical city, summer in Kaohsiung gets quite brutal, but winter is normally very mild, nice, and pleasant.

我在南台灣的高雄出生，高雄市台灣的第二大城市。我從小就 是個城市女孩，我喜歡熱鬧的感覺，而高雄就是這樣的地方。高雄有一些有名的夜市，也很靠近迷人的海灘。因為高雄位於熱帶，夏天可是熱得很，但是冬天通常也不太冷，很舒適怡人。

Cameron 卡麥倫

I was born in Chia-yi before my family moved to Taipei. Chia-yi is a small town south of Taichung. Chayi is famous for the turkey on rice and the beautiful sunrise in Ali Mountain, one of the major attractions in Central Taiwan. One thing people don't realize about Chia-Yi is how cold it gets in winter because we get cold breezes from the mountains.

在我家搬來台北之前，我是在嘉義出生的。嘉義是台中南邊的一個地方。嘉義有名的火雞肉飯還有迷人的阿里山日出，那可是中台灣有名的景點。大家通常不知道嘉義的冬天非常的冷，因為有山區的寒風吹下來。

Unit 2 Housing 房屋

Q2 What kind of housing do you have?

MP3 002

你家裡是住怎樣的房子？

We have a three-bedroom apartment in a 15 story building. There is a little space in the apartment itself, but we do have a large public area with an outdoor communal pool and an indoor gym. I love going down for a swim on Saturday afternoon because the hot chick from 12 B likes to hang out by the pool.

我們家在一棟 15 樓的大樓裡，是一間三房的單位。屋子裡的空間不是很大，可是公共區域倒是蠻大的，有個公用的室外游泳池還有室內的健身房。我最喜歡星期六下午去游泳因為 12 樓 B 座的美眉都是那個時候去。

Currently, I am renting the top floor out from a lady who owns a 3 story town house right next to Xindian MRT station. It is quite an old building, but the rent is surprisingly cheap compared with central Taipei. The decoration of the house is very dated, and there are a few issues with the plumbing, but as long as it is not haunted, I can live with a few leaking pipes.

目前我跟我的房東太太承租一棟三層樓透天厝的頂樓，就在新店捷運站旁邊。那是一棟很舊的房子，可是租金跟台北市中心比起來真的便宜很多。房子的裝飾很過時，而且家裡也有管線漏水的問題，可是只要沒有鬧鬼，我是不太介意滴水的問題啦。

Mom and Dad worked really hard to own our flat. It is on the 5th floor, but there is no lift in the building. We are planning to move to somewhere on the ground floor because my mum's got arthritis and her knees are getting worn out. Walking up and down the stairs everyday is killing her.

我爸媽很辛苦地買下我們住的公寓，公寓位在 5 樓可是沒有電梯。我們在想是不是要找個位在一樓的地方搬，因為我媽有關節炎，她的膝蓋快不行了，每天要走樓梯爬上爬下真的要她的命。

Unit 3 Building 建築物

Q 3 Can you recommend an interesting building in your home country to the tourists?

MP3 003

能推薦我你國家的一棟建築物給觀光客？

Sure thing! It would have to be the 85 Sky Tower in Kaohsiung. It is more than just an ordinary skyscraper. It is a shape of a castle to be exact and situated in the Kaohsiung harbour. The outside architectural glass reflects the view of the harbour. It looks amazing during sunset. Nothing can really top that!

當然可以！我會推薦高雄的 85 大樓，它跟一般的摩天大廈不同，它的外觀像一座城堡而且坐落在高雄港邊。外觀的玻璃帷幕反射著海港的景觀，日落的時候看起來真是美呆了！沒有什麼比那更好了！

It might not be everyone's cup of tea, but I will recommend the waste incinerator in Bei-Tuo, Taipei. The incinerator is a 150 meter tall chimney with a revolving restaurant on the roof top and a viewing platform. I recommend visitors have a meal in the restaurant as long as they can get over the idea of having a meal on top of piles of rubbish.

我想推薦的建築可能有些人沒辦法接受，那就是北投的垃圾焚化爐。它的外觀像個 150 公尺高的煙囪，頂樓卻有個旋轉餐廳還有觀景台。如果大家不排斥坐在滿坑滿谷的垃圾上吃的東西的話，那我會建議旋轉餐廳用個餐。

Cameron 卡麥倫

Yes, the first thing to come to mind is the Lan Yang Museum located in Yi-Lan county. What makes it interesting is, it looks like a tilted building and half of it has sunken into the lake, you think you are seeing the other half that is emerged on the water. The design is so clever, and I have never seen anything else like it.

可以，我第一個想到的建築物是位在宜蘭的蘭陽博物館。它最有趣的地方是建築物本身看起來像一座半倒的建築，而其中一半沉在湖裡。你會覺得你看到的是浮出水面的一半，它的設計真的很特殊，我從來沒有看過這樣子的設計。

Q 4 What is your favourite restaurant?

MP3 004

你最喜歡去哪間餐廳吃飯？

I love going to the buffet restaurant in Hyatt hotel. They have the best selection of seafood and good range of carvery. Their oysters are absolutely to die for! I don't go there that often because it is quite pricy, probably only for special occasions like my birthday. I think to indulge yourself once a while is pretty reasonable!

我最喜歡去凱悅飯店吃自助餐了！他們的海鮮種類很多樣，爐烤肉塊的選擇也還不少。他們的生蠔超美味的！我是不太常去吃，因為實在還蠻貴的，大部分都是特殊節日像生日之類的才會去。偶而犒賞一下自己也不過分吧！

Most people might give me a hard time about the choice of food, but my favourite restaurant is actually KFC, I go there at least once a week. I know fast food is not good for you, but their fried chicken is just so irresistible! I do try to health it up by getting salad instead of chips. It makes me feel less guilty for eating junk food!

大部分的人聽到我最喜歡的餐廳都會皺眉頭，可是我真的很喜歡肯德基，我至少一個星期去一次。我知道速食對身體不好，可是他們的炸雞真的很難抗拒！我會把薯條換成沙拉來均衡一下，這樣我也比較沒有吃垃圾食物的罪惡感。

I must tell you about this restaurant called Buddha's hand. Their vegetarian food is top shelf! I go there with my family when we have visitors. My favourite dish is the sweet and sour monkfish. The monk fish is crispy on the outside and soft in the centre. It is amazing! I mean, with food like that, it is actually not so bad being a vegetarian.

我一定要跟你推薦這家叫"佛手"的餐廳，他們的速食真的非常棒！我家如果有客人來的時候，都會去那裏吃飯。我最喜歡的那道菜是糖醋素魚，素魚炸的外酥內軟，真的很美味。其實如果吃的是這樣的菜色，那吃素真的一點也不痛苦。

Q5 Can you recommend a park for family with young kids?

MP3 005

你可以推薦一個適合有小孩的家庭去的公園嗎？

I think Kenting National park is great for kids of all ages. There are natural reserves up in the hilly area for kids who like bushes and hiking. And if they are into watersports, Kenting National park is right next to the beach. Young kids can have a splash by the beach and older ones can go for snorkelling or surfing if they are adventurous.

我覺得墾丁國家公園最適合小孩了，不管是大小孩還是小小孩。喜歡爬山健走的可以到山丘的自然公園去走走。如果喜歡水上活動的直接到墾丁國家公園的旁的海灘，小小孩可以玩玩水，大一點愛刺激的還可以去浮潛或是衝浪。

It would have to be the Central park in Kaohsiung. The park is totally designed for kids, there is a playground, and a water fountain, and small maze. The best part is the bird life there. There are lots of pigeons and ducks by the pond. I was lucky I didn't get pooed on! I think a family with young kids would really enjoy it.

那一定是高雄的中央公園了！這個公園完全為小孩設計的，有遊樂場，噴水池還有一個小迷宮。最特別的是這裡鳥類很多，池塘附近聚集的很多鴿子還有野鴨，還好沒有鳥在我頭上大便。我覺得有小孩的家庭一定會很喜歡這裡。

Cameron 卡麥倫

I would recommend Da-An Forest Park in Taipei. Here are slides, swing sets, and a large jungle gym. It is difficult to find a decent park for kids in Taipei because of the value of the land. I am glad at least the kids got a nice park to go to.

我會推薦台北的大安森林公園。有溜滑梯，盪鞦韆還有很大的攀爬設備。在台北因為寸土寸金，所以很難找到適合小孩的公園，還好至少有它們這個地方可以去。

Q 6 When was the last time you visited a museum?

MP3 006

你上次去博物館是什麼時候？

Only two weeks ago when my cousins came down to Kenting to visit us. We took them to National museum of Marine Biology & Aquarium in Ping Tong. We had a great time learning about different types of corals and fishes from different parts of Taiwan. I think the place is really well set up. It is both fun and educational.

我兩個禮拜前才去過，我表弟他們來墾丁找我們時，我們帶他們到屏東的海洋生物博物館。我們學到很多跟珊瑚有關的知識，還有台灣海域不同的魚種。我覺得海生館設計得很好，讓人覺得很好玩也很有教育性。

I think it was a few years ago when I first moved to Taipei. My family and I took a trip to National Palace Museum to check out all the treasures that Chiang Kai Shek allegedly took with him to Taiwan when he lost the war with Chairman Mao. There are some really awesome things there, and my favourite is the piece of jade that looks like a piece of stewed pork.

好像是幾年前我剛搬到台北的時候，我跟我家人到故宮去玩。去看看傳說中國共內戰蔣公撤退台灣時，從大陸運來的寶物。實在有很多稀世珍寶，可是我最喜歡的是一塊看起來像滷肉的玉石。

I think the last time would be when I was on a school excursion to the National museum of Nature Science in Taichung. The memory is a bit vague, but I still remember the big dinosaur skeleton in the main entrance, I thought that was so cool whenI was a kid!

我想最後一次去應該是國中時到台中科博館戶外教學的時候。我的記憶已經很模糊了，我只記得入口的地方有一個很大的恐龍骨架，我小時候覺得那很酷。

Unit 7 Hotel 飯店

Q 7 How do you choose a hotel when you are on holiday?

MP3 007

你去度假的時候會選擇住怎樣的旅館?

I always go for Youth hostel or back packer's hostel if I am on holiday. Normally, they are not far from the hustle and bustle. I am looking for people to party with and the guests there are normally looking for a good time, too! I am not picky about the facility, as long as it is clean and functional.

我度假的時候不是選擇青年旅館就是背包客棧，通常那些旅館都離熱鬧的地方不遠。我也是想要找志同道合的人一起去跑趴玩樂，大部分的住客也都是這種心態。硬體設備如何我是不太介意，只要乾淨能用就好。

I normally travel on a shoe string budget, so the cheaper the better is what I say. But I don't like to share a room with strangers, so I would look for a small hotel with maybe two or three stars. If you look hard enough, there are some really good bargains online if you book early.

我通常預算都很低，所以越便宜越好。可是我又不喜歡跟陌生人同住一室，所以我大概都找一些小的二星或三星飯店。如果你努力一點找，通常網路上都有一些很便宜的早鳥專案。

I like to spoil myself a bit when I am on holiday. I worked hard to save the money for the trip, and I just want to reward myself. I like a fancy place preferably with an outdoor pool and breakfast.There is nothing better than waking up to a breakfast buffet.

我度假的時候喜歡享受，畢竟錢是我辛苦工作賺來的，回饋一下自己有什麼不對。如果價格可以接受的話我喜歡高級一點的地方，最好要有室外游泳池還要含早餐。誰不喜歡早上起床就有豐盛的自助早餐吃。

Unit 8 Sport Center 活動中心

Q 8 Do you exercise in a sport center?

MP3 008

你會去活動中心運動嗎?

No, not really, because the sport center does not really offer things that I like to do. I am more an outdoor person than an indoor person. I like open water swimming and diving which are not something you can do indoors. Nothing beats the smell of the ocean and the wind blowing on my face

沒有，並不會，因為活動中心並沒有我喜歡的運動項目，而且我喜歡自己去。我是一個很愛戶外運動的人，我喜歡到海裡游泳還有潛水，這些都不能在室內進行。我最享受大海的味道還有暖風吹在臉上的感覺了！

I actually do, I take hip hop classes in China Youth Corps Center every Thursday night. The fees are affordable and facility is quite good, too. The most important thing is, the instructor is really hot, he's got a really nice six pack. I love it when he gives me the one-on-one attention and personally shows me the moves!

其實有，我每個星期四晚上都在救國團的活動中心上嘻哈舞課。學費便宜而且設備也還不錯，最棒的是教練很帥，他的腹肌好性感。我超愛他單獨過來一對一指導教我怎麼跳！

Yes, I do. Once every couple of months I will go to the baseball batting cage to practice batting. It is good fun but I can't afford to go every week, it just gets too expensive. Most of the weekend I just practice with my friends in the local school field.

有，我會去。每隔幾個月我就會去棒球打擊練習場練習擊球。是很好玩可是我沒辦法每個星期都去，實在負擔不起。大部分的周末我都是跟朋友在附近的學校操場練習。

Unit 9 Outdoor Space 戶外地點

Q 9 Where is your favourite outdoor space?

MP3 009

你最喜歡的戶外地點是哪裡？

Josh 喬許

There are lots of beaches in Kenting, but my favourite spot is the beach called Bai-sha which means white sandy beach in Chinese. It is a secluded area hidden among the palm trees. If you have watched the movie "Life of Pi" you would have seen the beach already, it is where Pi was washed up from the ocean.

墾丁有很多海灘，可是我有個最愛的景點叫白砂，白砂中文的意思就是白色的沙灘。那是一個隱密的地方，被層層的椰子樹圍住。你如果看過電影「少年 Pi 的奇幻漂流」那你就知道那個地方長什麼樣子了，就是 Pi 被沖上岸的那個的地點。

Abby 艾比

My favourite outdoor place would have to be the roof top of my building. It is like my secret hideout as well. I love to go up there just to chill out and do a bit of gardening to tidy up my pot plants. It calms me right down.

我最喜歡的戶外景點就是我家的頂樓了！那也是我的私房景點，獨處的地方。如果我很想放鬆的時候我就會上頂樓澆澆花，整理一下盆栽。這使我冷靜下來。

Cameron 卡麥倫

I love the hot springs in Bei-Tou, and my favourite outdoor hot spring is in this boutique hotel. Their hot spring area literately hangs off the cliff, and you feel like you are surrounded by mountains when you are in it. I love taking my girlfriend there, it is perfect for couples, the view is unbelievable!

我喜歡北投的溫泉，而且我發現了一個泡溫泉最棒的地點，就是這間精品飯店。它的溫泉區就是真的是懸掛在山邊，在那裡你真的可以感受到群山環繞的感覺。我最喜歡帶我女朋友去那裡，很適合情人去，景色實在太美了！

Unit 10 Neighbor 鄰居

Q 10 Do you like your neighbors?

你喜歡你的鄰居嗎？

MP3 010

Josh 喬許

My neighbors are nice people, but sometimes I really want to avoid them. Most of them are old ladies around my mother's age, they love gossiping and are always strying to play matchmaker. They all tried to set me up with girls when I was single, I am sure if they found out I've got a steady girlfriend, they would hassle me to get married every time they see me.

我的鄰居人都不錯可是有時候我真的想躲她們。她們大部分都是看著我長大的，跟我媽年紀差不多的太太們。她們真的很八卦而且很愛幫人做媒。我單身的時候每個人都想幫我介紹，我如果跟她們説我有女朋友了，她們一定一天到晚催我結婚。

Abby 艾比

I don't have much to do with my neighbors because I am always at work, and I have been moving around a bit since I moved to Taipei. I know they have a couple of young kids and they do get a bit noisy now and again, but there is no drama. I stay up late anyway, so they wouldn't keep me awake.

我跟我鄰居不太熟，因為我大部分時間都在加班，而且我搬到台北之後也常搬家。我知道他們有兩個小孩，有時候會有點吵鬧，可是沒有什麼大問題。反正我也都很晚睡，不會吵到我。

Cameron 卡麥倫

Yeah, I get along well with my neighbors. Mrs. Huang next door is my favourite because she is forever bringing us stuff. She makes the best rice dumplings. I always look forward to tasting her dumplings for dragon boat festival.

是的，我跟我鄰居們很好。尤其是隔壁的黃媽媽，我最喜歡她了。因為她常常會帶東西給我們，她包的粽子真的超好吃的！我端午節最期待的就是吃她的粽子了。

Unit 11 Teacher 老師

Q11

MP3 011

Have you ever been inspired by a teacher?

曾經有老師讓你覺得受到他的感動及啟發嗎?

Josh 喬許

I was once told by my English teacher that I would never make it through high school because I never handed in any homework. I used to hate her, but when I got older, I am actually quite thankful for what she said because I worked twice as hard just to prove her wrong, and look at me now!

我以前的一個英文老師跟我説我高中應該畢不了業，因為我從來不交功課。我曾經很討厭她，可是等我長大一點之後，我其實還蠻感謝她的，因為我為了證明她是錯的，我真的加倍努力，才有現在的成就。

Abby 艾比

Most of the teachers I had just seem to take teaching as a job. I don't think they would go the extra mile to encourage students to achieve their potential, at least not to me. It is a bit unfortunate, I couldn't think of anyone that inspired me.

我遇到的老師大部分都沒什麼熱忱，教書對他們來說好像只是一份薪水而已。我覺得他們不太會特別用心去鼓勵學生，激發他們的潛力，我遇到的都是這樣。也算我運氣不好啦！這樣來說的話，沒有唉，我沒有遇到這樣的老師。

Yes, there are a few actually. I consider myself pretty lucky that I was surrounded by teachers with passion and kind words throughout my school life. I always remember when my math teacher pulled me aside and told me I should pursue my studies overseas, that is what I am working towards.

有，其實有好幾個。我覺得我的求學生涯還蠻幸運的，我身邊的老師們都很有熱忱而且都很會講鼓勵人的話。我一直都記得，我的數學老師曾經把我拉到一邊私底下跟我說，我應該出國留學，這也是我一直追求的目標。

Unit 12 Ideal partner 理想情人

Q12 What do you look for in an ideal partner?

MP3 012

你心中的理想情人應該是怎麼樣的?

I think my ideal partner would have to love outdoor sports as much as I do because I want to be able to share my passion with her. A hot beach babe would be the type of girl I normally go for, but my mother might not agree with me on that one.

我的理想情人應該要跟我一樣熱愛戶外活動，因為我想要有一個可以分享相同興趣的伴侶。海灘辣妹是我最喜歡的型，可是我媽就不覺得她們適合我。

I would love to meet a guy who is nice and sweet, tall and handsome with charming eyes. I don't mind his background as long as we can talk to each other and being on the same page about what we want in life. I think Orlando Bloom from Lord of the Rings would be a perfect one! I just can't resist a clean-shaven guy.

我希望有一天我可以遇到一個溫柔體貼的男孩，最好是高大帥氣還有一雙迷人的眼睛。我不太介意他的背景如何，只要可以溝通，心靈相通，對未來的想法一樣就好。我覺得如果像魔戒中的奧蘭多布魯那就太棒了！我最喜歡斯文型的男生。

Cameron 卡麥倫

I thought I would prefer a quiet person like me, but I found I am always attracted to girls who are outgoing and bubbly, I guess it is just to make up for my shortcoming. Maybe someone from a similar educational background, so we will have something in common to talk about.

我以為我自己會喜歡跟我類似的人，可是我發現我卻覺得外向活潑的女生很吸引人，應該是跟我互補吧。如果跟我有類似的教育背景的話我們就會更有話說。

Unit 13 Friend 朋友

Q13 Please describe a close-friend.

MP3 013

請形容你的一個好朋友

Josh 喬許

It would have to be my buddy Dylan. I grew up with Dylan because he is my next door neighbor, he is like the brother I never had. We both love outdoor sports. I talk to him about everything, and he knows all my secrets!

我想說我的麻吉狄倫，我跟狄倫從小一起長大，他是我的隔壁鄰居，我一直把他當親兄弟看。我們兩個都喜歡戶外活動，也都一直念同一所學校。我跟他無話不談，我的秘密他都知道。

Abby 艾比

Tina is a friend of mine, I met her at the Hip hop class. She also really enjoys dancing. We hang out a lot at the weekend because she also doesn't have a boyfriend. I did not realize she actually knows my brother until I added her as a friend on Facebook. What a small world.

我有一個朋友叫婷娜，我在嘻哈舞課認識她的，她也很喜歡跳舞。我們週末常常一起出去，因為她也沒有男朋友。我加她臉書好友的時候才發現原來她認識我哥。這世界真小。

My best friend from high school is called Ah-Hsiung. We love to play basketball together. He is tall and skinny like a stick, but his build is perfect for basketball. All the juniors go crazy for him when he is playing. He was so popular when we were in high school, and he still is now with the ladies.

我高中的好朋友叫阿雄，我們很愛一起打籃球。他又高又瘦像根竹竿一樣，可是這種身型很適合打籃球。只要他一上場全部的學妹都會為他加油，他高中時代很受歡迎，他現在還是很受女生的青睞。

Q 14 Do you like children?

你喜歡小孩嗎？

MP3 014

I love kids, especially my five-year-old nephew – Jordon. Jordon is great. He loves surfing as much as I do. He is very talented. I always take him to the beach on Sundays and teach him how to surf. I can't wait for him to grow up and be my surf buddy!

我超愛小孩的，尤其是我五歲的外甥喬丹。喬丹很棒，他跟我一樣愛衝浪，他也很有天分，我每個星期天都帶他到海邊教他衝浪。我好期待他趕快長大，可以當我的衝浪夥伴！

Yes, I do. I am very close to my nieces; I volunteer to pick them up from school everyday because my sister can't get off work in time. I really enjoy spending time with them. They get excited about the simplest thing. It is such a pleasure to see the smiles on their faces.

嗯，我喜歡。我跟我的姪女們很好，因為我姊來不及下班去接他們，我都自願去接。我很喜歡跟他們在一起，他們可以因為很沒什麼的事情就很高興，我很喜歡看他們的笑臉！

Cameron 卡麥倫

Honestly, I am a bit scared of kids actually because I don't know what to say to them, and every time I try to play with them, they just end up in tears. I tried very hard to be a popular uncle but no matter what I do, it just wouldn't work.

說真的，我其實有一點怕小孩，因為我不知道要跟他們說什麼。每次我過去跟他們玩，都會把他們弄哭。我也很想當個受歡迎的叔叔，可是就沒辦法。

Unit 15 Animal 動物

Q15 What is your favorite animal?

MP3 015

你喜歡什麼動物?

I would love to have a pet chameleon; I think it would be really cool! They look kind of scary, and people often think chameleons are ferocious, but they are actually quite tame. They don't really bite unless they are agitated. They eat with their tongue just like frogs. I don't own one because they are just too hard to look after.

我很想要有一隻變色龍，我覺得它很酷！他們的外型有點嚇人，讓很多人覺得變色龍很兇猛，其實他們很溫馴。除非他們被激怒了，不然不會咬人。他們跟青蛙一樣用舌頭吃昆蟲。我並沒有真的去養因為他們蠻難照顧的。

Zebras are my favorite animals. I like the black and white stripes on them. Every time I see one I always try to figure out whether it is a white zebra with black stripes or a black zebra with white stripes. I was told a herd of zebra is called a dazzle because their pattern can actually dazzle the predators' eyes when they gather in large numbers.

我最喜歡的動物是斑馬，我喜歡他們身上的條紋。每一次我看到斑馬我都會仔細的看他到底是有黑條紋的白馬還是有白條紋的黑馬。有人跟我說一群斑馬是用 dazzle 這個字來形容，原因是他們一大群聚集在一起的時候，身上的條紋會讓掠食者眼撩亂。

I love dogs. I think dogs are not only human's best friend.They are also very useful with their excellent sense of smell. Labradors are calm and friendly. They are used as guide dogs. Beagles are used in the airport to detect drugs and prohibited items. I have a lot of respect for dogs.

我喜歡狗，我覺得狗不但是人類最好的朋友，他們靈敏的嗅覺對人類的貢獻很多。就像拉不拉多既穩重又友善，他們可以當導盲犬。米格魯在機場用來偵測毒品還有違禁品。我對狗這種動物很感恩的！

Unit 16 Relatives 親戚

Q16 Do you stay in touch with your relatives?

MP3 016

你跟你的親戚們會保持聯絡嗎？

It is hard not to stay in touch with your relatives especially when you are from a small town like Heng Chuan. Most of my relatives are my neighbors, and I go to school with some of my cousins, too. I couldn't get away from them even if I wanted to!

不跟親戚聯絡實在太難了，尤其是像我住在恆春這種小鎮。我大部分的親戚都住在附近，我跟我的表兄弟也上同一間學校。就算我不想跟他們聯絡也是會遇到。

Not really. I personally don't really make any effort to stay in touch with my relatives. It is more my mum's job. She is the one that calls everyone up during Chinese New Year to say hello, but sometimes you can't even find them. One of my uncles borrowed lots of money from my dad then he ran off. There is no way to contact him anyway.

不太會，我個人是不會主動跟我的親戚聯絡，那都是我媽的事。她過年都會跟他們打個電話問好，可是有時候還找不到人呢！就像我一個叔叔跟我爸借了錢就跑路了，根本就找不到人。

I am quite close to my cousins because we are all about the same age, although they live in Chia-yi still, there is Skype and LINE. I talk to them quite often.

我跟我的表兄弟們很好因為我們的年紀很接近，雖然他們還住在嘉義。可是現在有 Skype 還有 LINE 很方便，我們常常聯絡。

Unit 17 Weather/season 天氣/季節

Q17 What do you like to do in your favorite season?

MP3 017

在你最喜歡的季節裡你最喜歡做什麼事？

I love Summer; I think my skin tone says it all! I love spending time under the sun to build a nice tan. Trust me, the ladies love it! I always volunteer to do beach watch in Summer because I get to look cool in my board shorts and show off my muscles!

我最愛夏天，看我的膚色也知道。我喜歡在戶外曬太陽，曬成古銅色。相信我，女生都很吃這套！我夏天常常自願到海邊去當救生員，因為我可以正大光明的穿著我的海灘褲秀肌肉！

My favorite season is autumn because it is the best season to enjoy crabs. My favorite thing to do is to go to a seafood restaurant with my family and order seasonal made-to-order stream crabs. We will pay more to order the female crabs because the crab roe is just to die for!

我最喜歡的季節是秋天，因為秋天的螃蟹最肥美！我最喜歡做的事就是跟我家人到海鮮餐廳去點季節限定現點現做的清蒸秋蟹。我們情願付多一點錢要母蟹，因為蟹黃蟹膏真是太美味了！

Cameron 卡麥倫

I love Winter, and I love going to the hot spring then because it is just so comforting. Hotsprings are very good for your health. The proper way to do it is to soak in the hot spring first then jump into the cold one for a brief moment. Repeat that a few times, it really clears your head.

我最愛冬天了，而且我喜歡冬天去泡溫泉因為真的很療癒。其實泡溫泉對身體很好，泡溫泉正確的方式是先泡溫泉，然後簡短地泡一下冷泉，這樣重複幾次，真的讓人神清氣爽。

Unit 18 School days 求學生涯

Q18 What was your favorite subject in your school days?

MP3 018

你求學過程中最喜歡的科目是什麼?

Josh 喬許

My favorite subject is biology. I really enjoy learning about animals, insects, and the structure of the human body. My favorite part of the class is the lab work where you get to dissect a frog to see how the muscles work. I still recall some of the girls in my class got so scared of the muscle reflex.

我最喜歡的科目是生物，我很喜歡學跟動物、昆蟲還有人體構造有關的。課堂上我最喜歡的部分是到實驗室去解剖青蛙看肌肉的運作方式。我還記得我們班上的一些女生被肌肉的反射嚇得半死。

Abby 艾比

I love geography the most. My geography teacher from junior high school was really funny. He made geography really interesting. He would get us to pretend we were planning a trip to a certain area or country, and I actually learnt a lot from the class. What a brilliant way of teaching!

我最愛上地理課了，我國中的地理老師是個很有趣的人，他讓地理變得很有趣。他會叫我們搜集要到某個地區或是國家玩的資料，我在課堂上學了很多，這種教法真的太聰明了！

I really like art classes because I get to do what I like to do. Preparing for the university entry exam was a stressful time. I always look forward to art class, so I can take my mind off things. However, art class in high school doesn't really teach you much technique.

我真的很喜歡美術課，因為我可以做我喜歡的事。準備大學聯考是壓力很大的，只要到美術課我就很高興，因為我可以暫時不用想讀書的事。可是高中的美術課並不會教你什麼畫圖的技法。

Q19 Have you ever taken any talent class

MP3 019

你曾經學過什麼才藝嗎?

Josh 喬許

I actually took some Latino dance classes when I was little. I was getting pretty good at it. My speciality is the Cha Cha Cha. I didn't want to continue because I was worried about being judged by my friends. You know how 8-year-old boys are like!

其實我小時候學過拉丁舞。我的恰恰還真的跳得不錯。可是我沒有再繼續學下去因為我怕被我的朋友們笑，你知道八歲的小男生就是這樣啊。

Abby 艾比

I did Karate when I was in elementary school. I didn't want to do it, but my father wanted me to be able to defend myself from bullies, and he is a firm believer in martial arts. I went along with it for a few years, but I was never any good.

我國小的時候學過跆拳道，我不想學，可是我爸說我一定要學會保護自己，不要被霸凌。他對武術這方面是深信不疑，我順著他的意學了幾年，可是沒學到什麼。

Cameron 卡麥倫

I started to learn how to do proper oil painting since I was 10 years old. I have always been artistic and gifted in painting when I was little. My parents have been very supportive, and they decided to enroll me into the oil painting class although I was the youngest student among them.

我從十歲就開始正式的學油畫，我一直都是比較有藝術細胞的，對畫畫這方面很有天賦。我父母親一直都很支持我，所以他們決定送我去油畫班，而我是全班最小的學生。

Unit 20 Driving 開車

Q 20 Do you prefer driving or walking?

MP3 020

你喜歡開車還是走路？

I think it depends on where I am going. If I am only going to the corner 7-11 to get some beer, I much prefer walking to driving since you don't have to worry about parking. The journey is too short for a car ride.

那要看我要去哪裡，如果我只是要去轉角的 7-11 買啤酒那我走路就好了，因為我也不用擔心停車的問題，路程這麼短，根本不需要開車。

I actually don't own a driver's license which leaves me with no options other than walking or taking public transport everywhere.You wouldn't want to drive in Taipei anyway. Parking is a pain in the ass to find and even if you do find a space, it will cost you an arm and a leg.

其實我連駕照都沒有，所以也沒得選擇，不是走路就是坐大眾交通工具。在台北你也不會想開車的，車位難找的要死，就算找到了也是貴得很。

Cameron 卡麥倫

I prefer driving for sure because I need to visit my clients regularly at the industrial park outside of the city. I don't know any other way to get there other than driving! I know finding a place to park the car is a potential problem, but being punctural is my priority. There is no other way.

我一定選擇開車，因為我常常需要到近郊的工業區去拜訪客戶。如果不開車我還真不知道我能怎麼去。我知道找車位可能很難找，但是我不準時不行，也只能開車了。

Q 21 What do you normally do for your birthday?

MP3 021

你通常都怎麼慶祝生日？

My birthday is a big thing. My friends like to make a big deal out of it. We will normally go somewhere for dinner before heading to the clubs. By the end of the night, we will be so wasted and can't even recall what we did and where we went! But it is always a night to remember.

我的生日是件大事，我的朋友們很喜歡高調慶祝。我們通常會先去吃飯，然後再到酒吧去，我們會盡情狂飲，到最後都不知道我們到底做過什麼去過哪裡，而且絕對是不醉不歸！

Normally, I will bring a cake to work to share with my coworkers because we get along really well. My boss doesn't normally get in until lunch time, so we are free to do what we want in the office. Some of us might go out for dinner after work, but that's about it.

我通常會帶個蛋糕到公司跟同事一起慶生，因為我跟他們很好。而且我老闆通常午餐時間才會進公司，所以我們蠻自由的。下班後可能跟幾個同事一起吃飯，但大概就是這樣了。

My mother is pretty traditional when it comes to my birthday; she insists on making me the pig knuckle noodle soup every year although she knows most likely I would have made dinner plans with my girlfriend to celebrate. However, I would always finish the noodle soup before I go out because I don't want to make her feel bad.

説到我的生日我媽是蠻傳統的，她總是堅持要煮豬腳麵線給我吃，雖然她知道我應該已經跟女朋友約了要出去吃飯慶生。我一定會先吃完她煮的麵線再出去，但那也是她老人家一番心意。

Unit 22 Accident 意外

Q 22 What would you do if you got into a car accident?

MP3 022

你不小心出車禍時會怎麼處理？

I will first check whether it is my fault or his negligence and whether we need an ambulance or not. If it is just a small bump or a scratch, I will just negotiate with the person and sort it out there and then. It gets too complicated when you get the police involved.

我首先會判斷是我的錯還是對方的失誤，看看我們需不需要救護車。如果只是小擦撞，那我就會跟對方商議是不是能在現場賠償解決就好，叫警察來實在太麻煩了！

I would totally freak out! I don't have a driver's licence, so I think if I did get into an accident I would be the victim. I guess there is not much I could do, if I got hit by a car, I just hope someone would call the police and the ambulance for me!

我真的會完全嚇壞，我沒有駕照所以我想如果我出了車禍，那我一定是被撞的那個人。我猜如果我被撞了，那我也沒有辦法做什麼事，可能要靠好心人來幫我報警還有叫救護車了。

I will call the police for sure because I need the police report to show my insurance agent. I have full coverage for the car and third party insurance. I think I am pretty much covered! I just hope I don't accidently kill someone, then it would be a real nightmare.

我一定會馬上報警，因為我需要給保險公司看報案紀錄。我的車有保全險，而且還有第三人保險，我覺得我沒什麼好擔心的。我只希望我不要意外撞死人就好，那就糟糕了。

Unit 23 Work/study 工作/求學

Q 23 What do you do?

你目前是做什麼的？

MP3 023

I graduated from university last year with a bachelor's degree in Physical training. At the moment, I am in the process of getting my application together for the master's degree in Sport Science in the University of Sydney. I hope they will offer a place to me, I can't wait to go surfing in the world famous Bondi beach!

我去年由體育系畢業，目前我正在準備申請雪梨大學運動科學的碩士學位。希望他們會收我，我迫不及待地想去世界出名的邦代海灘衝浪！

I am a procurement representative in this trading company called "CandyCan". "CandyCan" specializes in importing of European sweets and confectionary. The best thing about being in this industry is that you get samples for free. I literally get endless supply of the finest Belgium Chocolates.

我是一家叫「糖罐子」的貿易公司的採購專員，「糖罐子」是專門進口歐洲的糖果糕餅。做這份工作最好的地方就是廠商會寄樣品給我，我常常收到比利時的高級巧克力呢！

I am a sales engineer in a company called Sinclair. Sinclair is a production line machine supplier. My job is to look after my clients and provide them with the technical support and parts. The most annoying thing about my job is that I have to be available on the weekends, too.

我是辛克萊爾的銷售工程師，辛克萊爾是生產線機器的供應商。我的工作是照顧我的客戶，提供技術支援還有零件供應。這份工作最討厭的地方就是我週末也要待命。

Unit 24 Travel 旅遊

Q 24 Do you travel a lot?

你常去旅行嗎？

MP3 024

I did a fair bit of travel in Taiwan with my classmates I have been to most of the famous tourist attractions in Taiwan. The most memorable trip was my surfing competition in Tai-dong last year. I was so close to winning a prize.

我以前常跟我的同學在台灣到處跑，台灣大大小小的旅遊勝地我大概都去過，可是記憶最深刻的還是我到台東參加衝浪比賽那一次，我差一點就有獎可以拿。

I don't often go on big trips because it is hard to take time off work. I do like to go overseas, and I have been to Japan and Korea. Sometimes I will go out of my way to visit a place recommended by travel books. But I found most of the time, those places are not as good as how it is described in the book.

我不太常有機會去很久，因為我的工作很難請假。我是蠻喜歡出國的，我去過日本跟韓國。有時候我會特別去旅遊書上介紹過的地方看看，可是我發現那些地方實在沒有書上說的那麼好。

Other than going to the hot springs in Yang Ming mountain, I don't think I travel a lot. I do prefer to hang around the city. Maybe I will go to a different part of the town and try a new café or a new restaurant. That is probably as adventurous as I get.

除了到陽明山泡溫泉之外，我好像沒機會到處去。我其實也比較喜歡在市區晃。偶爾我會到平時很少去的區域去走走，試試看沒去過的咖啡店或是餐廳，這樣對我來說就算是旅行了。

Unit 25 Sport event 運動比賽

Q 25 Do you like to watch sports events live?

MP3 025

你喜歡看運動比賽的實況轉播嗎？

Absolutely! Nothing is more exciting than a live sports event. I would go to a stadium if I could, but I don't live in New York, so there is no way that I can watch the Yankees play in person. Live TV broadcasting is the next best thing! I normally watch the games with my friends in the house.

那當然！沒有什麼比看現場比賽更刺激的了！如果可以的話，我當然想去體育館看現場，可是我又不住在紐約，沒有辦法現場看洋基隊比賽，能有實況轉播就很不錯了！我通常會到我朋友家跟他一起看。

Well, I am not a sports person, watching a sport event live would be a torture for me. I don't get excited like the fans. I mean if it is an important sports event like the Olympic, I would be curious about whether Taiwan has won a match, but I wouldn't stay up the whole night just to watch it live.

這個嘛，我不是很愛運動的人，看現場的運動比賽簡直就是要我的命，我不像運動迷們心情跟著起伏。如果是重要的比賽像奧運之類的，我當然會關心台灣是贏還是輸，可是我絕對不會熬夜來看實況轉播。

I do like to watch live sports events, but most of the time I've got to work the next day, so I don't have the luxury to stay up late to watch the games. If I knew the game was going to be on in the early evening, then I would make an effort to watch it live.

我喜歡看實況轉播可是大部分的時間我隔天都要工作，所以不太可能有這個閒暇時間不睡覺來看比賽的。如果我知道轉播的時間是在下班時間以後的話，那我就會看轉播。

Unit 26 Weekend/free time 周末/休閒

Q 26 What do you normally do in your free time?

MP3 026

你有空的時候通常會做什麼?

If the weather is good, then I will be at the beach, but if the weather is not right, then I will be at home playing video games! Video games are so addictive, so I lose track of time so easily. I can keep playing the whole night, if my mother didn't come and stop me.

如果天氣不錯的話，那我就會去海邊，可是如果天氣不好，那我就會在家打電動。電玩這種東西真的很容易讓人上癮，我一開始打就會忘了時間，如果我媽沒有來叫我的話，我可以一直打下去。

I will go shopping if I am free the whole day on the weekends. But if I only have an hour here and there, I watch Korean soaps instead. I stream them online, and I normally watch one or two episodes then I have to force myself to turn it off. Otherwise, I would run out of internet data in no time!

如果我週末整天有空的話我就會去逛街，可是如果我只有零散的一兩個小時，那我就會上網下載韓劇。我通常只會看個一兩集就強迫關機，不然下載的容量很快就用完了。

Juggling between my girlfriend and my jobs is really tiring. My favorite thing to do in my spare time is actually doing nothing, just chilling out or catching up on sleeps.

平常要陪女朋友又要上班真的很累。我有空的時候最喜歡就是懶在那裡什麼都不做，不然就是補眠。

Unit 27 Color 顏色

Q 27 Do you prefer to wear dark colors or light colors?

MP3 027

你比較喜歡穿深色或是淺色的衣服？

I prefer to wear light colors, such as white or bright green. I spend a lot of time sun-bathing to get the tan I want, and I like to wear something that would complement my skin tone. I think light colors represent my personality as well. I am energetic and always positive.

我喜歡穿淺色的衣服，像白色或是很亮的綠色之類。我好不容易才把我的皮膚曬成我想要的膚色，我當然要選擇可以襯托我膚色的顏色。我覺得淺色也很可以代表我的個性，我一直都是很有活力而且很正面的。

I think it depends what kind of mood I am in. If I don't have any formal things to attend on that day, I prefer to wear a light color. But if I have a formal meeting or something important on, then I prefer to wear a dark color just to look more professional.

我覺得要看心情，如果我今天沒有什麼重要的事要處理，那我就想穿淺色的，可是如果我有會要開或是有重要的事，那我會選擇深色，這樣看起來比較專業。

I would prefer to wear dark colors because I need to visit my clients in the factory, and I'm very likely to get grease or dirt on my shirt. If I wear a dark color shirt, I can hide the stains pretty well, but with a light color shirt, you can spot the stain from miles away. That's what I try to avoid.

我會喜歡穿深色，因為我常需要到廠房裡見客戶，廠房裡到處都是油汙，常會弄到衣服。所以如果我穿深色的，那污漬就看不太出來。如果換成是淺色衣服的話，那遠遠的就可以看到汙漬，我會盡量避免。

Q 28 How often do you use a computer?

MP3 028

你用電腦的機會多嗎?

Josh 喬許

I had to use a computer almost everyday while I was a student, but since I graduated last year I have been spending lots of time at the beach. My computer is sitting on my desk gathering dusts as we speak. I hardly touch it now, and I check all my emails on my smartphone anyway.

我還沒畢業之前我很常用電腦，可是去年畢業之後我大部分的時間都在海邊，我的電腦現在就丟在桌子上埋在厚厚的灰塵底下。我現在很少開電腦，我都用智慧型手機來看電子郵件。

Abby 艾比

I use a computer everyday at work for the correspondence between the company and our overseas suppliers. I will be in so much trouble, if the internet was not working because all emails would not come through properly. I can't live without the computer. I stream all my Korean soaps online with my laptop, too.

我在公司每天都要用電腦跟國外供應商們連絡。如果網路當掉的話我就糟了，因為不知道是不是每封郵件都有收到。我沒有電腦就會活不下去了，因為我的手提電腦是拿來下載韓劇用的。

I don't use the desktop often but rely on my smartphone a lot because I am out and about visiting clients all the time. I do have to input the orders into the computer just for record keeping once every couple of days.

我不常用我的桌上型電腦，可是我很常用智慧型手機，因為我幾乎都在外面見客戶。我大概每隔幾天就要開電腦一次來輸入這幾天的訂單。

Unit 29 Movie 電影

Q 29 What kind of movie do you like the most?

MP3 029

你最喜歡看哪一類型的電影?

I like to have a good laugh, so comedy is always my go-to. My favorite is the "Hangover". It is about a group of friends deciding to go to Vegas to celebrate the stag's night. They accidently got drugged, so they had no recollection of what actually happened the night before. All they know is the groom is missing, and they have to find him in time for the wedding. It is hilarious, you've got to watch it.

我覺得人生就是要開心所以看電影我也喜歡看喜劇。我最喜歡的騙子就是「醉後大丈夫」。這部片子是在講有關一群朋友決定到拉斯維加斯去慶祝單身的最後一夜，但是他們卻意外地被下藥完全不記得前晚發生過什麼事。他們只知道新郎不見了，一定要把他在婚禮前及時找回來。故事內容超搞笑的，大推！

I love girly movies, a sweet love story would be ideal. I also prefer a happy ending because most of the love stories in real life do not have fairytale endings. I think movies should not be too close to reality because life is hard enough as it is, why watch something that reminds you of how terrible life can be!

我喜歡浪漫愛情片，最好就是很甜蜜的故事。我也喜歡皆大歡喜的結局，因為現實生活中很難真的有童話故事般的愛情。我覺得生活既然都那麼苦悶了，電影劇情就不應該太寫實，不然看了心情更糟。

Cameron 卡麥倫

I am a big fan of special effects and science fiction; I cannot resist the Si-Fi movies, such as “Starwars” and “Avatar.” I think watching movies is a way to escape from reality, I always try to imagine I am one of the characters while I am watching the movie.

我超愛看有特效的故事，像「星際大戰」或是「阿凡達」那種科幻片我一定會去看。我覺得看電影就是要有想像空間，我總是一邊看一邊幻想我是電影裡的主題人物。

Unit 30 Vehicle 交通工具

Q 30 Do you own a vehicle?

你有沒有自己的交通工具?

MP3 030

Yes, I do. I have a scooter, and in southern Taiwan that is all you need. There is not a lot of traffic in Heng Chuan, and unless you are going out to the town; otherwise, you don't really need a car. Scooters are perfect because they have very good fuel economy, and you don't need to worry about the parking.

有，我有。我有一台機車。在南台灣機車就很夠用了。在恆春也沒有車潮，除非你要到別的縣市去，不然你也不需要開車。機車就最適合了，又省油又不用擔心停車的問題。

Well, I don't own a car or a scooter, but I do have a push bike for my exercise routine on the weekends. Personally, I think there is no need to own a vehicle when you live in a city like Taipei. Owning a vehicle is more a hassle than a convenience when parking costs more than food!

嗯，我沒有房車也沒有機車，可是我有一台腳踏車，是我用來周末假日健身用的。以我個人來說，我覺得我並不需要有車，尤其是住在像台北市這種地方。有車其實弊多於利，停車費比便當的錢都還貴呢！

Cameron 卡麥倫

Yeah, I've got a small car. It is a 2014 Mitsubishi Coltplus. I drive to work everyday, and all I need is a small car which is good on fuel. I bought it second-hand from a car yard, but it comes with a 6 months warranty. I bought it a year ago, and it hasn't caused any problems.

有的，我有一台小車。是 2014 年的三菱 Colt plus 車款。我每天都需要開車上班，所以省油的小車最適合我。我是在二手車場買的，還有含六個月的保固。我買了一年了，到現在都沒什麼問題。

Unit 31 Song 歌曲

Q 31 Do you like to listen to love songs?

MP3 031

你喜歡聽情歌嗎？

Love songs are not my cup of tea. I find most of the love songs are just corny and predictable. Either you like that girl but the girl doesn't love you back, or you are happily in love with someone. I am not ready to settle down with anyone just yet I guess that's why I can't really relate to it.

情歌呢，真的不是我的菜。我覺得大部分的情歌都很老套又一成不變，不是你愛那個女孩而那個女孩不愛你，就是目前戀愛 ING。我目前還不想定下來，可能是這樣我對情歌真的沒什麼感覺。

I love the love songs because I always imagine I will meet my Mr. Right one day and live happily ever after just like what the lyrics say. Obviously, my Mr. Right is still waiting to be found, but listening to love songs keeps me positive about finding true love one day.

我很喜歡聽情歌，因為我總是幻想著有一天我會遇到我的真命天子，過得幸福美滿，就像歌詞裡寫的一樣。雖然我的真命天子目前還沒出現，可是聽著情歌會讓我對未來充滿希望，我相信我總有一天會找到他的！

I don't mind love songs because some of them really touch my heart especially when my ex-girlfriend decided to walk out on me a couple of years ago. I was very upset because we were almost engaged. Sad love songs did save me from the misery.

我不介意聽情歌，因為有些歌我覺得寫得很好，很有共鳴。尤其是幾年前我剛跟我前女友分手的時候，我很低潮，因為我們差一點就訂婚了。聽傷心的情歌來抒發心情，我也慢慢走出來了。

Unit 32 Photograph 照片

Q 32 Do you prefer to take photos of others or being in the photo?

MP3 032

你比較喜歡照相還是幫人拍照？

Well, I spend a lot of time and effort making sure I look the way I am, of course I would like to show off my looks as much as I can. I update my Facebook profile photo everyday with my daily selfie! Some people might think I love myself a bit too much, but I love being in photos.

嗯，我花了很多時間與精力來維持我的外表，我當然想曝光率高一點啊！我每天都會上傳自拍照更新臉書的大頭照，有些人覺得我實在太自戀了，可是我真的很喜歡看到我自己的照片。

Taking photos to me is like creating memories for different occasions. I cherish every moment with my friends and family, and I like to be in the photos with them. I like to print the photos out and look at them from time to time. People always remember who is in the photo, but no one remembers who took the photo!

我覺得照片是用來留下回憶用的，我很珍惜跟家人朋友在一起的時刻，所以我喜歡跟他們一起出現在照片中。我會把照片都洗出來，偶爾會拿出來翻閱。大家都只會記得照片中的人，不會有人記得照片是誰照的！

I don't like being in the photos because I think I am not photogenic at all. To be honest, I think I look terrible in most of my photos although my mother says I look good. I much prefer being the photographer instead. I think taking photos of nice plates of food is much more fun than taking photos of myself.

我不喜歡出現在照片中，因為我很不上相。雖然我媽都說照片很好看，可是說真的我覺得我每張照片都很醜，所以我情願當幕後的攝影師，我覺得拍食物都比拍我自己來得有趣。

Unit 33 TV program 電視節目

Q 33 What is your favorite TV program?

MP3 033

你最喜歡看什麼電視節目？

I love to watch American TV series. My favorite show is "Friends". It is not the latest series, but it is the classic all-time favorite. It is all about love triangles and friendships among 6 friends. The storyline is funny and easy to follow. The best thing is, I picked up a lot of slang from watching the series.

我很愛看美國的電視影集，我最喜歡的是「六人行」。這不是最新的，但卻是最經典，最受人喜歡的一套影集。內容是有關這六個好友之間的感情糾結還有誠摯的友誼。劇情很好笑，也很容易看懂。最棒的是看了這個影集我還學到很多英文的俗語。

My favorite program on TV is actually the shopping channel. I know they are just sales presentations, but I like to know what is the in thing at the moment. If I saw something I like, I would order the product because they offer 10 days free trial and guarantee your money back. There is no risk of wasting money, other than the hassle of arranging for return collection.

我最喜歡的電視節目其實是購物頻道，我知道那不過就是賣東西而已，可是看一下現在在流行什麼也好。如果我看到我喜歡的東西，我也是會買，因為它有十天鑑賞期，還保證退款，我覺得沒什麼浪費錢的風險，只是要安排退貨比較麻煩而已。

I like to watch the News channel because I think the Taiwanese News channel is quite entertaining. The news coverage not only includes serious stuff like suicide bombing, but also funny stories like where would be the best spot for Pokemon Go! I watch news everyday, so I won't run out of conversation topics with my clients.

我喜歡看新聞台因為我覺得台灣的新聞台很有娛樂性。新聞裡不只有像人肉炸彈這種嚴肅的新聞事件，還會告訴你寶可夢要去哪裡抓比較好。我每天都會看新聞，這樣我才有話題可以跟客戶聊天。

Unit 34 Fashion/clothing 時尚/服飾

Q 34 What type of clothes do you normally wear?

MP3 034

你平常的穿著打扮是怎樣？

I pretty much wear T-shirt and board shorts everyday because I don't need to worry about dressing up for work. The weather in Heng Chuan is always hot and humid, even the winter is really mild. All you need is a long sleeve jacket. I do have a wind breaker for my scooter ride. I don't think I own a lot of thick winter clothing.

我幾乎每天都是 T 恤加海灘褲，因為我不需要去上班要穿什麼。而且恆春的天氣又濕又熱，就算冬天也不是太冷，大概加件長袖夾克就可以。要騎機車的時候我會穿風衣，我其實沒什麼冬天的衣服。

I normally wear a dress to work on week days, but on the weekends I like to wear something more casual, maybe shorts and a singlet. If the weather is a bit windy then, I will put on jeans and a slim fit jacket. I like wearing high heels because it just looks sexy.

如果是要上班的時候我通常是穿洋裝，可是週末的話我就穿得隨便一點，大概是細肩帶上衣加熱褲。如果風有點大的話，我就換牛仔長褲還有合身的夾克。我還喜歡配高跟鞋因為我覺得看起來很性感。

Business shirt with workpants is my standard outfit because I need to look professional for work. If I need to go and visit clients, then I might put on a tie. I don't often wear a jacket because it is too warm in Taiwan. I get really sweaty if I wear one.

我的標準穿著就是襯衫加西裝褲，因為上班的關係，需要穿得正式一點。如果我還需要去見客戶的話，那我會再加條領帶。我通常不會穿西裝外套，因為台灣的天氣實在太熱了，我如果穿的話會汗流浹背。

Unit 35 Food 食物

Q 35 What is your favorite food?

你最喜歡吃什麼東西?

MP3 035

I love to go to this hawkers' food stall right by Heng Chuan bus terminal because they got the best oyster omelette. They get the freshly harvested oysters from Tong Kang everyday, and they have a secret recipe for their omelette sauce. I go there at least once a week.

我最喜歡恆春車站旁邊的小吃的蚵仔煎，他們的蚵仔煎最棒了！他們每天都從東港運來現撈的鮮蚵，再加上他們的特殊醬料，我至少一個星期要去報到一次。

I actually really like fried chicken and chips. I know they are not the healthiest choices for food but they are just so tasty. Most of the time my diet is pretty healthy. I eat plenty of fresh fruit and vegetables but when I feel like a midnight snack, that is the first thing that comes to mind.

我其實很喜歡吃炸雞跟薯條，我知道這很不健康可是他們真的很美味。我大部分都吃得很健康，我吃很多新鮮蔬菜跟水果。可是如果有半夜嘴巴有點饞的時候，我第一個想吃的就是炸雞跟薯條。

Cameron 卡麥倫

My favorite food is dumplings. I like them whether they are fried, steamed, or boiled. My favorite flavor is the pork and chive one. It goes really well with a bit of soy sauce and vinegar dipping sauce. Some people like to add fresh ginger to the sauce, but I just find it too strong.

我最喜歡吃餃類了，不管是煎餃、蒸餃還是水餃我都喜歡。我最愛的口味是豬肉韭菜，這跟油醋醬油沾醬很搭。有些人喜歡加一點新鮮的薑絲，可是我覺得這樣味道太濃了。

Unit 36 Game 遊戲

Q 36 What was your favorite game when you were little?

MP3 036

你小時候最喜歡的遊戲是什麼？

Josh 喬許

My favorite game was hide and seek. We used to play it with all the kids from the neighborhood in front of the temple. I was pretty good at the game. I loved to hide right behind the big banyan tree, and the funny thing is that no one seems to know to look there!

我以前最喜歡玩躲貓貓了，我常常跟鄰居的小孩們在廟口玩。我還蠻厲害的，我最喜歡躲在大榕樹的後面，很奇怪就沒人會去那裏找。

Abby 艾比

When I was little, I loved to play tea parties with my sister, we would bring out all the bears and dollies and pretend they were guests in our castle. We would dress them up as princesses and feed them imaginary cake or biscuits. It sounds silly now, but I loved it when I was a kid.

我小時候最喜歡跟我妹妹玩家家酒，我們還會把小熊跟娃娃都拿出來把他們當成來訪我們城堡的客人，我們還會幫他們穿衣服，扮成公主，再請他們吃假裝的蛋糕還有餅乾。現在說起來好像很蠢，可是我小時候真的超愛的！

Cameron 卡麥倫

I always carried marbles with me when I was little. I was obsessed about playing marbles, I took them everywhere with me. I still remember I played marbles with my classmates during recess at school everyday. I had a whole collection of them, big ones and little ones, you name it.

我小時候隨身都會帶著彈珠，我真的很迷打彈珠這回事，無論到哪裡都堅持要帶著。我還記得每天只要下課鐘聲響，我就會跟同學去玩彈珠。我蒐集了很多彈珠，有大的有小的，只要你說的出來我幾乎都有。

Part 2

話題卡回答

- **釐清思緒：** 掌握大原則，口說話題總離不開食、衣、住、行、育、樂，系統式備考雅思。

- 掌握備考關鍵，備考不茫然無助，釐清考試脈絡後，迅速攻略口說話題，巧取雅思口說高分。

新聞故事

請描述一段讓你覺得印象深刻的新聞故事

新聞一｜日本的猴子愛泡溫泉 Hot spring monkeys

在日本北海道有一個奇觀，就是雪猴泡溫泉。因為氣候寒冷，冰天雪地裡雪猴群們也就地取材，一隻隻跳進現成的溫泉裡。溫泉裡的猴子有大有小，完全不怕人。他們臉上的表情真的好享受，真是蔚為奇觀。沒有親眼目睹還真是難以想像。

新聞二｜載大熊回家 The giant Teddy

幾年前有家賣場推出巨大的絨毛玩具熊，一隻只要台幣一千塊。很多年輕人瘋狂搶購，這也造成了騎機車載絨毛大熊回家的窘境，還有人因為車裡塞不下，直接把熊綁在車頂。回到家更糟糕，發現熊太大沒位子放，又要載回去退錢！

Q1 Describe a story you heard or read about in the news that made an impression.

MP3 037

請描述一段讓你印象深刻的新聞故事

印度能吃的餐具 Edible cutlery

I read this story in the newspaper once. This Indian inventor created an edible spoon which is made of a combination of millet, rice, and wheat. It looks just like a normal wooden spoon, but it is totally biodegradable.

我曾經在報紙上讀到，有一個印度的發明家，他用小米、白米還有麥子混和做出了可以吃的湯匙。那個湯匙看起來跟一般的木湯匙沒兩樣，可是卻是可以腐化分解的。

He first got this idea from knowing how much plastic cutlery is wasted each year and it just keeps piling up. Plastic does not degrade in a natural environment, plus, it is not as safe as we thought because plastic

他靈感的來源是發現原來一年裡面被丟棄的塑膠餐具這麼的多，而且數量每一年不停地增加。塑膠在自然環境裡面不會

is a chemical complex. Toxic substances will be released into food when the conditions are right, such as high temperatures or contact with oil.

腐化分解而且塑膠也不是我們想像中的那麼安全，因為那是種化學合成物，毒素會藉由高溫或是跟油質接觸時而溶解到食物裡。

Therefore, an edible cutlery would be just the solution. His edible spoons even come in different flavors to compliment different dishes that you can choose from: plain, sweet or savory. I think it is really clever!

所以發明可以吃的湯匙就是最好的解決辦法了。他的湯匙還有分不同口味來搭配不同的食物，有原味、甜的或是鹹的，我覺得實在很酷！

However, his business did not take off rapidly. Although he has the perfect recipe and idea to make edible cutlery, the cost of the making it is so much higher than making plastic cutlery. India is known as a poor country; the majority of the popula-

可是他的生意並沒有大展鴻圖，雖然他有很棒的配方和想法來做出可以吃的餐具，可是他卻沒有辦法把這個餐具做的跟塑膠餐具一樣便宜。

tion cannot afford edible cutlery. He would have to market his environmental friendly product to a different consumer group.

在大家印象裡，印度是一個蠻窮苦的國家，大部分的人口負擔不起可以吃的餐具。他必須要另外找客戶群。

I think he should promote the idea in the western countries where there is more environmental awareness. It might make his business more sustainable.

我覺得他應該到西方國家去推廣，他們也比較有環保意識。這樣他生意才可能可以持續下去。

湖泊/河川：水漾森林

請描述一個你曾去過或是想去的湖泊或河川

湖泊一｜嘉明湖 Chia-Ming Lake

我從高中時期就一直想去嘉明湖。嘉明湖位於台東縣，它有個很美的名字叫天使的眼淚，因為不管從哪個角度看，湖面總是湛藍的。可是因為嘉明湖有很多可怕的鬼故事，所以我也一直約不到人可以一起去挑戰。不知道這輩子會不會有機會去。

湖泊二｜曾文水庫 Tseng-Wen Reservoir

我國小的時候因為參加童軍團的關係，曾經去台南縣的曾文水庫露營。曾文水庫是台灣最大的人工湖，也是影響嘉南平原供水的重要水庫。壩頂的風景很壯觀，群山環繞非常的美麗。我印象最深刻的是滿天星斗的夜晚，那是我第一次看過這麼多星星。

Q2 Describe a lake or river that you have visited or want to visit.

MP3 038

請描述一個你曾去過或是想去的湖泊或河川

水漾森林 Mystery swampy forest

There is a secret location in Chai-Yi County near Ali Mountain that not many people know about. There is this beautiful dammed lake that was caused by the 921 earthquake. What's special about this lake is, the trees were trapped in the flood slowly losing their leaves and dying eventually, and all the dead tree trucks stick out of the lakes like the telephone poles. It looks amazing with the blue sky and the reflection of the lake. People call this place "Mystery swampy forest." Around 10 years the club members of mountain hiking were planning a trip to the "Mystery swampy forest."

在 921 大地震後，嘉義縣阿里山鄉出現了一個秘境，一座因為地震阻斷溪流而產生的堰塞湖，這個湖特別的地方是，湖裡原有的樹因為泡在水裡而死亡，只留下一根根像電線桿的樹幹從水中竄出，配合藍天及湖水的倒影，大家稱這個地方為水漾森林。

I was very tempted, but unfortunately it was only open to club members, so I missed out on the opportunity.

大概是十年前我還在念大學的時候，登山社的同學計畫要到水漾森林去。我很有興趣可是因為只有開放給社員，所以我就錯過了。

I was told you have to be fit to be able to make it because it would take 5-6 hours on foot in the winding mountain trail and occasionally there are vertical climbs.

有人告訴我要去水樣森林需要很有體力，因為大概要走5-6小時的山路，偶爾還有垂直的攀爬。

I am quite a small person, and I doubt if I would be able to carry all the gear with me and walk such a long way. I know the view would probably be worth it, but the moment I think I have to walk another 5-6 hours to get back. The reality starts to sink in.

我不算高大，我懷疑我真的有辦法背那麼重的行囊走那麼遠嗎？我知道美景應該很值得看，可是一想到回程又是5-6個小時，我就怕了。

I watched a documentary about it not long ago, and it was saying the water level there is dropping dramatically. I do wish I could visit the lake before it disappears completely.

不久前我看了一段紀錄片，說水漾森林的水位急速減少，我希望在它完全消失之前有機會去看。

電器：智慧型手機

請描述一樣讓你生活更便利的電器

電器一｜電腦 computer

現在的學生應該連打字機長什麼樣子都沒看過，其實就是桌上型電腦的前身。電腦真的是跨時代的發明。現在生活中的每個環節幾乎都跟電腦有關。就連去餐廳吃飯，也是用電腦點餐。電腦可以互相連線，對於資料的整合實在太方便了，不用人工一個一個比對。

電器二｜行動電源 Power bank

行動電源對我來說太重要了！我這種整天滑手機的人，電池根本就不夠用。以前我隨身帶電源線，只要有機會，不管到哪裡都會把手機拿出來充電。自從有了行動電源之後，我就不用到處找插座，這樣我女朋友也不會找不到我了！

Q 3 Please describe a piece of electronic equipment which made your life easier.

MP3 039

請描述一樣讓你生活更便利的電器

智慧型手機 Smartphone

Where shall I start with my smartphone? A smartphone is everything in one! It is a phone, a camera, a calculator, a computer and so much more !

我該從何說起呢？智慧型手機簡直是集所有優點於一身，它是手機，也是相機，計算機還是台電腦呢！還有其他數不清的功能。

I was not a smartphone user until pretty late. I was a bit resentful about learning new technology.

我不是一開始就是個智慧型手機的支持者，剛開始我也很排斥新科技。

Before I got my first smartphone, I didn't understand why people get

在我拿到第一支智慧型手機之前，我

addicted to their phones, but now I can't live without my phone.

不懂為什麼有人會對手機上癮，可是我現在真的不能沒有我的手機。

I have to check my emails when I am out and about for work.I had to bring my laptop with me everywhere I went before, but all I need now is my smartphone. If I want to scan some information to share with my coworker, all I have to do is take a photo with my smartphone, then send it as an attachment in my email. This is definitely revolutionary!

我在外面出差時需要不斷地察看電子郵件，以前我到哪裡都一定要帶我的筆記型電腦，現在我只需要我的手機，就算我需要掃描文件給我的同事看，我也只要拿手機照張相，然後用郵件附件傳出去。這真是太劃時代了！

My favorite function is skype. I can check on my boyfriend all the time. If I wasn't sure whether he is telling me the truth, I will get him to put skype on, so I can see where he is. Who would have thought this is

我最喜歡的功能其實是 Skype 視訊，我隨時隨地都可以查我男朋友在哪裡。如果我覺得他沒有講實話，我就叫他

what I use Skype for!

開視訊，讓我看看他在哪裡。沒有人想到視訊可以這樣用吧！

But the thing is, convenience does not come cheap. I spent about 1000 NTD a month on phone bills; otherwise, I would not have enough data to do what I want to do. Luckily, I am not obsessed about having to have the latest model; otherwise, it would cost more!

可是科技的方便性真的不便宜，我一個月大概要花台幣一千元來繳電話費，不然我的網路容量不夠。還好我是不堅持一定要最新款的手機，不然開銷會更大！

重要的決定：唸哪個科系

決定一｜結婚 Marriage

跟女朋友交往五年了，去年她一直催我結婚，其實我也是很想娶她但是我一直覺得我的工作向來不穩定，養家是很大的責任。她一直說她年紀到了，不趕快生她會變成高齡產婦。我爸媽也覺得早點定下來是好事，我們就決定結婚了，目前我覺得還習慣這種生活。

決定二｜辭職 Resignation

大學畢業後好不容易找到一份工作，雖然不是理想的工作，但是至少有一份穩定的薪水。不過我一直覺得同事在找我麻煩，老是嫌東嫌西。還在老闆面前說我不好。我撐了三個月到最後還是決定辭職，因為做自己不喜歡的工作真的是度日如年。

Q 4 Please describe an important decision in your life.

MP3 040

請描述一個你人生中重要的決定

念哪個科系 Choosing a major

I had a hard time making the decision about the major I'm going to take, knowing it would have a major impact on my career life in the future.

選科系的時候我實在很難下決定，因為我知道這會影響我未來工作的方向。

I always liked dancing and I always dreamed of being a professional dancer one day I have been taking dance classes since I was little, and I was pretty talented, too.

我一直都很喜歡跳舞，也想像有一天可以當個專業舞者，我從小就學舞，而且也蠻有天份的。

But when I started to look at the reality, I was not confident that I could make a living as a dancer. I know I am a good dancer and with more training, I would be an out-

可是當我想到實際面的時候，我實在沒把握當舞者可以填飽肚子。我知道我跳得很好，如果透過適

standing one!

當的訓練我會變得更傑出。

However, I think the reality of being a part of the entertainment business is pretty cruel. I am not the tallest or the finest looking dancer on the dance floor. I guess it kind of limited my opportunities.

可是娛樂業的現實面是很殘忍的，放眼看過去我也不是最高挑最漂亮的舞者，我看我還是算了。

It was a painful decision, but I decided to do commerce instead. I think commerce fits in this society better, and I also believe the salary of business related position would be able to support the lifestyle I want. I gave in to reality!

下這個決定實在很痛苦，可是我決定要念商科。因為商科的性質比較容易被這個社會接受。而且我也相信從商的薪水可以達到我想要的生活型態。我向現實屈服了。

I don't mind being in the ac-

我不介意現在在

counting firm, and I don't regret what I chose. But somehow I always wonder, if I ever did take up dancing, where would I be today？Maybe I would be performing on Broadway or being part of a dancing company touring the world！You just never know!

會計公司的職務，我也不後悔我的選擇，可是我偶而會幻想如果我當初選擇舞蹈系的話，現在會在哪裡？我可能會在百老匯表演，搞不好會跟知名舞團去世界巡迴表演！真的很難説呢！

音樂：韓國流行音樂

請描述你喜歡聽的音樂類型

音樂一｜交響樂 Symphony Orchestra

我很喜歡去音樂廳看交響樂團的演出，我覺得欣賞現場的音樂演奏表演很有震撼力。有些人可能會覺得交響樂很無聊，可是我覺得聽交響樂讓我的思路更清晰，我喜歡閉上眼睛仔細地聆聽旋律的起伏，陶醉在大提琴的低沉音符裡。

音樂二｜沙發音樂 Lounge music

我最喜歡沙發音樂，尤其是咖啡廳裡播放的沙發音樂，不知道是不是裝潢的關係，在那裡聽沙發音樂真的很舒服。我覺得沙發音樂讓人很放鬆，雖然沒有很強的節奏感，但是輕快的旋律讓我會不自主地跟著哼唱，一邊看雜誌一邊聽音樂真是享受。

Q5 What kind of music do you like to listen to?

MP3 041

請描述你喜歡聽的音樂類型

韓國流行音樂 K Pop

My favourite music would be K Pop. I think they have the best boy bands and girl bands in the world! Their songs are really catchy. You don't have to know Korean to know how to sing along for a few sentences, like "Gangnam style" by Psy and "No body" by the Wonder girls.

我最喜歡的音樂就是韓國流行音樂，我覺得他們的男子和女子樂團真是世界第一！他們的歌曲很容易琅琅上口，就算你不會韓文也可以跟著唱幾句，就像江南大叔的 Gangnam-style 還有 Wondergirls 唱的 Nobody。

I once watched this documentary about the inside of forming a Korean pop band. Not only do they want the band to be popular in Korea, their ultimate goal is to make

我曾經看過一段有關韓國團體的秘辛，他們的目標不只是要在韓國成功，最終目標是要把韓國流

Korean Pop music an international success.

行音樂推向世界。

To achieve that, the record companies have to make sure they have got the best cards in hand. Apparently, every single component is carefully thought out and executed, when it comes to a team member selection, training and most importantly, the song selection.

為了要達成這個目標，唱片公司必須要好好計畫，並確認每個步驟都做得正確。尤其是選擇團員，嚴格的訓練還有最重要的是歌曲的選擇。

How to make people who do not understand Korean to like Korean songs is one big challenge, if you pay attention to those popular Korean songs, you will notice they all have part of it in English.

要如何讓不懂韓文的人唱韓國歌曲可是個大挑戰，如果你仔細聽，你會發現他們的歌裡面都一定會有一段英文。

Apparently, hundreds of songs are discarded for every one song that is selected. This is how much ef-

而且他們是從幾百首歌中挑出一首歌，這就是他們對歌

fort they put in to make sure the song is right. I think K Pop is the whole package, the team members are expected to look a certain way too. So many fans are willing to go under the knife just to enhance their look to look more like their favourite pop star. I must say K pop does wonders to people!

曲選擇的用心。我覺得 K Pop是一種文化，所有的團員看起來都有種特定的樣子，讓很多歌迷更是不顧一切的去動刀，就為了讓自己看起來像喜歡的歌手。我只能說韓國天團還有讓人變美的神奇力量呢！

廣告：眼鏡公司廣告

請描述一段你覺得有趣的廣告

廣告一｜樂透彩券 Lottery

一對看起來很窮的父子在火車上，兒子看著沿途的風景，不斷地告訴爸爸他看到了什麼東西，例如說：房子跟汽車等等。爸爸就會反問他喜歡嗎？兒子就點點頭，爸爸手上拿著他剛買的樂透彩券，一邊笑著幻想著中獎之後他會有很多錢，他不停地跟兒子說，爸爸買給你！一券在手，希望無窮。

廣告二｜汽車廣告 Peugeot

一個印度型男因為嫌他的車款太舊，又負擔不起新車，所以他突發奇想，決定把舊車的外型用各種方式，例如向前撞牆把引擎撞凹，往後倒車把原本的房車撞成掀背車的後車外型。加上其他的敲敲打打，終於把他的舊車重新塑形為 Peugeot 的新車款，他很驕傲地開出去把妹。

Q 6 Please describe a TV commercial that you think is interesting.

MP3 042

請描述一段你覺得有趣的廣告

眼鏡公司廣告 SpecSaver

This commercial was created for a glasses company called SpecSaver in Australia. They were aiming to differentiate themselves as being more affordable than the others.

這個廣告是澳洲一家叫 SpecSaver 眼鏡公司的電視廣告。他們的訴求就是要以價格將他們與其他競爭者區隔開來。

One day, a son came to his elderly mother's house to visit her, and they are having tea and cake in the kitchen with the view of her garden. He noticed that she was wearing a new pair of glasses. He commented on how nice those glasses were, and it must have cost her a lot of money.

有一天兒子回家看媽媽，跟媽媽在廚房喝下午茶一邊聊天，他家的廚房看出去就是花園。他注意到他媽媽配了一副新的眼鏡，他稱讚那副眼鏡很好看，一定很貴吧！

She then replied and said, No, the insurance would cover it. Then the son started to question how expensive the lenses must be. She replied: It is 25% off on all lenses. I went to Spec Saver and don't you worry I am not spending your inheritance.

他媽媽回答：沒有，保險都有給付。兒子又說：那鏡片也一定要不少錢吧？媽媽回答：鏡片也都有打七五折，放心啦兒子，我不會隨便把你的遺產給花掉，我是去 SpecSaver 配的！

The son acted relaxed and said to her, Good! Then his mother said something that made him really worried. She looked through the window and said to him: Don't you worry, I am leaving them all to Derek. He turned his head then saw this hot, sexy and topless guy trimming the trees for his mother. The look on his face is priceless! He was in such shock.

兒子聽了就放心地說，那很好！結果沒想到他媽媽說你別擔心，我全部都要留給德瑞克！兒子轉頭順著他媽媽的視線看過去，沒想到看到一個沒穿上衣的性感猛男正在幫他媽修剪花園裡的樹枝。他真的臉都綠了！完全嚇傻了！

I think this commercial is simple but clever. The ending caught everyone by surprise. Viewers get the idea how competitive their price is straight away, but at the same time the commercial does not make Spec Saver seems like a cheap place. It still looks quite classy. I think that is why this commercial left an impression.

我覺得這個廣告拍得很淺顯易懂，結尾更是在大家的意料之外。觀眾看完就知道他們眼鏡的價錢很有競爭力，而且同時也不覺得SpecSaver 是一間很廉價的公司，還是蠻有品味的。這應該是我對這個廣告印象深刻的原因。

幫助：世界展望會

請描述一段你曾經幫助別人的經驗

經驗一｜喜憨兒基金會 Children Are Us foundation

每年母親節喜憨兒基金會的糕餅工廠都會推出送愛到部落的活動，除了訂一份給我媽媽之外，我都會多一份送給偏鄉部落的弱勢家庭。一方面是增加喜憨兒工廠的收入還有工作機會，另一方面是弱勢家庭也可以享受節慶的感覺，知道有人祝福著他們。

經驗二｜幫忙募款 Fundraising

莫拉克風災的時候雖然是台灣很痛苦的時期，但也感受到台灣的上下一心，真是有錢出錢，有力出力。我沒有辦法到南部災區去幫忙，所以我能做的就是幫忙募款。連續幾個禮拜我都跟著紅十字會的人拿著捐款箱到處去募款，我覺得很有意義。

Q 7 Please describe a situation when you helped someone.

MP3 043

請描述一段你曾經幫助別人的經驗

幫助他人 helping others

Ever since I got my first stable job, I said to myself that I want to do something for someone and pay it forward. I happened to see the campaign for World Vision and how they help out poor kids around the world. I decided to sign up with them as a sponsor. It does not cost much, only 7 hundred dollars a month, and it can change someone else's life completely. I think I can afford that!

自從我有第一份穩定的工作開始，我就跟我自己說要做些有意義可以回饋社會的事。我剛好看到世界展望會的幫助世界貧童的廣告，所以決定加入成為資助人。一個月才台幣 700 元就可以完全改變另一個人的生活，那我真的花得起這個錢。

The kid that was assigned to me is a five-year-old boy from Kenya. His name is Aton, and he has 5 other siblings.

我分到的兒童是一位五歲的非洲肯亞男童，他叫做阿堂，他的家有其他五個兄弟姊妹。

His parents do simple farming trying to support the family but with the weather conditions, what they get in return is not very much, and is totally not sustainable.

他爸媽只能種植一點簡單的東西來維生，可是因為氣候的關係收成很差，根本不可靠。

With my sponsorship, not only does Aton get the education that he needs, but also there will be regular food hamper delivered to his family. I think I help more than just one person.

因為有我的資助金，阿堂不只可以去上學，他們家也固定會收到糧食包。我覺得受惠的不只是他而已。

I have been doing it for over 10 years now, and I don't think I would ever stop being a sponsor.

我已經資助他十年了，我覺得我會一直資助下去。

I was just wondering what happens once Aton turns 18, does that mean he wouldn't need the sponsorship anymore? I guess they might give me another kid to sponsor since

我只是在想如果等阿堂滿18歲之後，展望會就不再資助他嗎？我猜他們應該會分另一個小孩給

there are so many kids in need especially in the third world countries. I really think it is meaningful to be a sponsor like that. I hope there will be more people who feel the same.

我吧，畢竟在第三世界國家需要資助的小孩是數以萬計。我覺得當資助人是很有意義的事，我希望會有越來越多的人跟我有同感。

書籍：人生不設限

請描述一本你喜歡的書籍或是雜誌

書籍一｜哈利波特 Harry Potter

雖然很多人覺得哈利波特是給小孩子看的，可是我覺得哈利波特的情節很引人入勝。故事內容主要是說哈利波特從小被阿姨一家人當成怪胎，直到他被帶入充滿魔法還有想像力的神奇世界，一連串的冒險情節，也解開了他的身世之謎。

書籍二｜富爸爸窮爸爸 Rich dad Poor dad by Robert T. Kiyosaki

這是一本財經書籍，但是他講的財經觀念，並不像一般高談闊論的財經書教你如何投資理財。作者用他本身的故事，他與他爸爸之間的互動來推翻找個穩定工作過一輩子的觀念。我覺得對即將出社會的學子們很有幫助，讓他們用不同的角度看賺錢這回事。

Q 8 Please tell me about a book or a magazine you like.

MP3 044

請描述一本你喜歡的書籍或是雜誌

人生不設限 Life without limits by Nick Vujicic

Speaking of Nick Vujicic who is the author of this book, I believe most of us have heard about him. He was born without limbs which is a rare form of disability. The book "Life without limits" is a reflection on his life, you can imagine being born with such a severe deformity, his life would not be smooth.

說到這本書的作者力克胡哲，應該沒有人不認識，他出生就沒有四肢，是一種罕見的病例。人生不設限這本書是他人生的回顧，可以想見他一生下來就有這麼嚴重的缺陷，他的人生一定充滿挫折。

I am not surprised he did attempt to end his life a few times since he was still a child. I feel really bad for him being forced to deal with teasing and scorn and bullied so badly at school. I mean I am a nor-

聽到他說小時候就有好幾次試著結束自己的生命，其實我並不驚訝。我覺得很難過他求學過程中被迫面對了多少輕蔑苛

mal kid, but I still get teased about being fat or ugly. I know what kids are like at school.

薄的言語還有欺負他的人。我也知道小孩就是這樣，我算是個正常人，都會有人說我肥或是醜了，何況是他。

It does take him quite sometime to realize that he needs to change his attitude if he still wants to live and he needs to turn his life around.

他也是花了不少時間才體會到如果他還想活下去，他需要改變現狀，他需要改變他對生命的態度。

My favorite quote in the book is: “Life without limbs or life without limits” and he did just that ! He knows he can’t sit around to wait for the miracle to happen for him, or he needs to turn himself into a miracle. How does he do that?

書裡我最喜歡的一句話是「到底要相信自己沒有手腳還是要相信自己潛力無限」他決定相信後者，既然等不到奇蹟出現，就把自己變成一個奇蹟吧！他是怎麼做到的呢？

First, he needs to learn to accept his condition and like who he is. Once he knows he needs to love and respect himself, he is fearless and driven to success.

首先他要接受自己的缺陷，當他學會愛自己，尊重自己之後，他就沒有什麼好擔心的了，可以盡全力去做到最好。

He is such an inspiration. I feel stronger and more confident towards things that I was too scared to try before. This book is highly recommended.

他的書很鼓勵人心，充滿了正面能量，看了之後我覺得我更有信心去面對我之前很恐懼的事。我很推薦大家去看這本書。

卡通/故事人物：海底總動員多莉

請描述一個你喜歡的卡通或故事中的人物

人物一｜藍色小精靈 Smurf

藍色小精靈的樣子很可愛，大部分的精靈們都是藍色的皮膚，戴一頂白帽子還穿白褲，再加上配件。其中我最喜歡小聰明，他除了戴帽子之外，還帶了一副眼鏡，每次都有好主意！故事裡的壞巫師想盡辦法想把藍色小精靈抓來吃，小精靈們個子雖小，可是每次都會同心協力的度過難關。

人物二｜多啦A夢 Doraemon

我最喜歡多啦A夢了，他是隻來自未來的機器貓。他的外型像兩顆藍色的球上下連在一起，圓滾滾的很可愛。他的任務是照顧他的朋友兼主人大雄，大雄一天到晚出錯，還好多啦A夢身上有個神奇口袋，無論是什麼危急的情況他都可以拿出不同的法寶來幫他的朋友們解圍。

Q 9 Please describe a character that you would like from a cartoon or story.

MP3 045

請描述一個你喜歡的卡通或事故中的人物

海底總動員的多莉 Dory

I love Dory from Finding Nemo. Finding Nemo is a story about a clown fish which accidently got caught by humans and his father searched everywhere he could trying to find him. The father clown fish named Marlin runs into Dory who helps him along the way to find his son. The duo went on an adventure across the 5 seas and finally found his son in Sydney, Australia.

我最喜歡《海底總動員》裡面的多莉，海底總動員是一個有關一隻小丑魚被人類抓走，而他的爸爸不停地搜尋只想找到他。這隻爸爸小丑魚叫馬林，他在途中遇到一隻叫多莉的魚，多莉沿途幫助他找他的兒子。這個兩人拍檔展開了橫跨五大洋的歷險記，到最後終於在澳洲雪梨找到他的兒子。

Dory is this blue fish with yellow fins, she suffers from short-term memory loss, but she never takes it as a problem! I guess her memory is just too short to remember it anyway!

多莉是一隻藍色帶有黃色鰭的魚，她常常只有短期失憶症，可是她從來不覺得這是個問題。我想也是，因為她根本記不得她有記憶的問題！

Most people would think she is just a forgetful and careless fish. But I see her differently. I think she is the eternal optimist, she is always so happy and excited about things.

大部分的人會覺得她是一隻健忘又粗心的魚。可是我不這麼想，我倒覺得她是終極的樂觀者！她對每件事總是那麼的正面，積極的去面對。

Her level of excitement is like she experiences things for the first time. I guess she is, because she can't remember she has done it before. Same as the frustration and disappointments, she doesn't hold

她對每件事的興奮程度就好像她從來沒做過這回事，我想也是，因為她不記得她有做過。同樣的，不高興或是失望的事

things against anyone because she can't remember what they have said or done to her any way. I guess it is probably not a bad thing to forget things that bother you after all.

她也忘得快，她對人沒有敵意，因為她早忘了別人是怎麼對她。我覺得忘記不好的事其實是件好事。

There is a sequel coming out about finding Dory this time. I am looking forward to seeing what happens after they found Nemo and how she got lost. I am sure it will be a great story!

海底總動員的續集要上映了，這次是有關尋找多莉的事。我很期待想知道他們找到尼莫之後多莉是怎樣不見的，這故事一定會很有趣。

名人：傑米奧利佛

請描述一個你欣賞的名人

名人一｜歐巴馬 Barack Obama

歐巴馬是美國第一任民選的黑人總統，我覺得很有劃時代的意義。他除了做政治決定很果斷之外，他私底下的作風卻是非常的親民，就像隔壁鄰居一樣。美國總統是可以影響世界的人，但他卻不會看不起白宮的清潔工，我知道他會是一個以民意為重的人。

名人二｜希拉蕊 Hillary Clinton

雖然她的夫婿柯林頓曾經任職美國總統，可是很多人卻覺得希拉蕊表現得比柯林頓出色。因為她的律師背景還有政治經歷都不輸柯林頓，她也一直位居要職，曾經當過美國的國務卿。2016年終於輪到她代表民主黨來選美國總統的大位。

Q 10 Please tell me about a famous person that you admire.

MP3 046

請描述一個你欣賞的名人

傑米奧利佛 Jamie Oliver

Jamie Oliver is someone I really look up to. There are lots of famous chefs in the world, but I think his belief makes him stand out from the rest. I think he is doing a lot of charity work through his ability to cook and understanding of food.

傑米奧利佛一直是我很欣賞的一個人，這世界上有很多出名的廚師，可是我覺得傑米的信念讓他與眾不同。我認為他是用廚藝的天分還有對食材的了解來做公益。

He knows everyone likes to eat, but not everyone knows how to eat well or what is good for them. He just wants to promote the idea of eating good food to avoid being overweight.

他了解大家都喜歡吃美食，可是並不是每個人都清楚怎麼樣吃才是對健康有益。他想要推廣吃好的食物而不是讓人會肥胖的食物。

He wants to help to rectify the problem of being overweight in the UK when he noticed the number of people suffering obesity in the UK is skyrocketing.

他注意到英國過重的人口年年遽增，而他想拯救肥胖的問題。

He soon realized that, the most effective way to rectify the problem is to educate the future generation to stop the trend of being obese. He initiated a program to visit school canteens to inspire the food provider to offer nutritious food instead of the junk food to the kids.

他腦筋動得很快，他發現最有效的方法就是從教育下手，讓下一代不要加入肥胖的趨勢。他發起了到學校去拜訪福利社的食品供應商，讓他們避免提供垃圾食物，盡量提供有營養的食物。

By the same token, he wants to take this opportunity to educate kids about what type of food is good for them.

他也順便趁這個機會教育學生，讓他們了解什麼叫做好的食物。

I think Jamie Oliver is trying to change the world with his own power and wanting to make an impact on people's perception of food which is a wonderful thing to do. I know it is impossible to change things overnight, but at least he is raising awareness and trying to reach out to his viewers.

我覺得傑米奧利佛是想用他的力量來改變人們對食物的觀念，我覺得這是件很值得讚揚的事。我了解改變需要時間，他現在開始提倡這個觀念至少可以影響到他觀眾群的層面。

節慶：清明節

請描述一個對你來說重要的節慶

節慶一｜復活節 Easter

復活節在台灣並不是很重要的節慶可是對我家來說倒是蠻重要的，因為我家是教徒。復活節的日期每年都不一樣，因為也是看農曆來決定。在復活節時，我們家也不吃紅肉，只吃海鮮來紀念耶穌受難日。教堂也會舉辦復活節的彩蛋活動，讓小孩們了解耶穌重生的故事。

節慶二｜聖誕節 Christmas

在台灣雖然聖誕節有放假，可是卻不是因為聖誕節的關係。我有參加教堂的唱詩班，聖誕節前夕我們會到附近的教友家傳福音。平安夜時我家人們會一起去參加午夜彌撒，教會也會安排愛心活動到孤兒院去發聖誕禮物給小朋友，我覺得很有意義。

Q 11 Please describe a festival which is important to you.

MP3 047

請描述一個對你來說重要的節慶

清明節 Tomb sweeping day

I would say Tomb sweeping day is quite an event in my family because we still have a few ancestors' plots in the cemetery where we go and pay our respects. One of the Tomb sweeping day traditions is to bring spring rolls as offerings.

清明節對我家來說還算是件大事，因為我們家還有幾門祖先的墓要去掃。清明節的其中一個傳統是要拜春捲。

My aunt will always prepare lots of food in her house, and the family will gather there for a big spring roll making spree before we head off to the cemetery. This is probably the only chance for me to catch up with my cousins and relatives from my father's side as well.

我嬸嬸總是會準備很多材料，大家會先在她們家集合做春捲，做完再出發到墓園去。這也是一年中難得的機會可以見到爸爸那邊的表兄妹還有親戚。

So Tomb sweeping is also a social occasion for us. Other than the spring rolls, we also need to have the gardening tools to get rid of the overgrown weeds, and also some ceremonial items, such as ghost money, incense sticks, and a set of colorful paper strips.

所以清明也是家族聚會。等我們做完春捲後，除了要準備園藝的工具來除掉高大的雜草，還需要帶祭拜用的東西，像紙錢、香，還有一疊彩色的壓墓紙。

We first do the general tidy up, and then we will put out offerings and set up the altar. When everyone is ready, we will light the incense sticks and burn the ghost money to greet our ancestors, to let them know their family is here to pay the respect and pray for good fortune.

我們首先會環境整理，再來把供品供桌弄好。等大家都差不多了，就點香燒紙錢向祖先膜拜，跟祖先說子孫們來看你們了，祈求祖先保佑。

The colorful paper strips are the final step of the ritual, they will be spread out evenly on the tomb and we will pin them down with rocks. It is kind of spooky because you have

壓墓紙是最後一道步驟，我們會把彩色的紙用石頭一張張分別地壓在整個墳墓上，其實有一點恐怖

to literally walk on top of where the coffin is buried top to place the paper strips. The colorful strips served as the decoration to show the others that this tomb is properly looked after by their family.

因為你在埋葬棺材的上方走來走去。壓墓紙算是一種裝飾，好讓別人知道這家的子孫有在照顧自己的祖墳。

Part 3

即席應答

- **殊途同歸**：有效拓展答題思路，其他口說測驗如新托福口說等亦適用。

- 所有話題亦與其他英語口說測驗的話題無甚分別，正所謂：一法通、萬法通，演練後面對各種話題均能有持無恐、游刃有餘。

Unit 01 Food

食物

Q1 Is Food safety becoming an increasingly serious problem in our lives?

MP3 048

食安問題逐漸變成我們生活中一個嚴重的問題了嗎?

I never thought food safety would even become a problem in the first place because food to me, is something that is safe to eat.

我從來沒有想過食品安全會成為一個問題，因為對我來說所謂食品都是安全無虞的，可以吃的東西。

Then after watching the news in the past couple of years, I was shocked by how much toxin we have been fed by those heartless, profit-

但是在看過這幾年的新聞事件之後，我無法想像我們到底被那些沒有良心，只

driven food manufacturers. It makes me wonder how much more there is to be discovered.

愛錢的商人們騙著吃進了多少毒素。我在想還不知道有多少事件要爆發呢！

I really think law enforcement should take some responsibility, too. The current food safety regulation is full of flaws, and the inadequate punishment and sentence length do not reflect the seriousness of their crimes. The food manufacturers often walk out clean which is very disappointing.

我覺得執法者也要負點責任，目前的食品安全法規充滿漏洞，罰則根本不成比例，還有罰則太輕，根本無法反映出罪行影響的層面有多廣泛。食品製造商也常常無罪釋放，這太令人失望了。

Q2 What do you think of organic food?

MP3 049

你對有機食品有什麼想法？

Some people think it is better for you and also better for the environment because organic farming follows a strict set of guideline on what pesticide and fertilizers are allowed to be used. I don't know whether it is necessarily better for the health, but what really concerns me is the rising price of groceries.

有些人覺得有機食品對身體比較好，也比較環保，因為有機耕種必須遵守嚴格的規定標準，尤其是農藥還有肥料種類的選用。我是不太曉得到底對身體是不是比較好，可是我的顧慮是物價的飆漲。

Organic food can cost up to 2-3 times more compared with food that was produced under the conventional methods. I would love to support the idea of organic farming, but I just don't think I can afford it unless my salary goes up to 2-3 times as well. Most of us grow up eating conventional farmed food, and it doesn't

有機食品的價格通常是一般傳統耕種食品的2-3倍。我是很想支持有機耕種，可是我覺得除非我的薪水也漲2-3倍，不然我根本負擔不起。大部分的人都是吃傳統耕種食物長大的，

seem to do us any harm. 好像也沒什麼不妥。

討論話題字彙

單字	音標	中譯
❶ sensible	[ˈsɛnsəbəl]	感知的
❷ element	[ˋɛləmənt]	要素
❸ temptation	[tɛmpˈteʃən]	誘惑
❹ integrity	[ɪnˋtɛgrətɪ]	正直
❺ unconventional	[ˌʌnkənˈvɛnʃənəl]	非傳統的
❻ inherit	[ɪnˈhɛrɪt]	遺傳
❼ dominating	[dɔmɪneɪtɪŋ]	佔主導地位的
❽ appreciate	[əˋpriʃɪˏet]	欣賞

Unit 02 Education

教育

Q1 What can schools do to help students to be more prepared in the next stage of their lives?

MP3 050

學校教育對於學生面對未來的人生可以提供怎樣的幫助？

I think Taiwanese schools tend to focus on academic performance rather than industrial related training and knowledge.

我覺得台灣的學校都傾向專注在學業成績而不注重產業相關的訓練或是知識。

I chose to do vocational training school instead where they provide more hands-on training than text-book learning. I still entered to uni-

我反而選擇職業學校，因為他們會提供實際產業相關的訓練而不是死讀書。我

versity after I graduated.

到最後還是上了大學。

I do think I have a better idea of what I want to achieve in the future compared with my friends who came through the conventional high school system.

可是我覺得我比我那些就讀傳統高中的同學們更有想法。

I chose to join the workforce instead of pursuing further studies because I actually felt I was ready to start working, and there is no need for me to obtain a master's degree to do the things I want to do. I think vocational training definitely helped me to know what I want to do.

我後來選擇不去念碩士，而是直接就業，因為我覺得我準備好要工作了，而我想做的工作並不需要碩士學歷。我覺得是因為念職校的關係讓我知道我要什麼。

Q 2 Do you think people are offered more opportunity in life if they have a qualification?

MP3 051

你同意學歷可以幫你打開更多機會的大門嗎？

Yes, I totally agree. I think qualifications are a ticket of entry to all kinds of opportunities. That is something that makes you stand out from all those candidates who apply for the same job. How does the employer know who is best suited for the job before they even meet you?

是的！我完全同意，我覺得學歷是一張讓你通往很多機會的門票。學歷會讓你在一群申請同一份工作的應徵者中一枝獨秀。老闆在還沒見到你本人之前怎麼會知道你適合這份工作呢？

To be good on paper is definitely an advantage to push you through to the next round which is the interview. But, how well you can impress the employer and whether you get the job, that's another question. When I apply for jobs, I often get called for

所以有好的學經歷真的可以幫你爭取到面試的機會，可是你能不能讓雇主喜歡你，或者能不能得到那份工作，這又是另一個問題了。說到應

the interview, but I don't always get that job. That's what makes me realise if it wasn't for the qualification, I might not even make it that far.

徵工作，我常常都會有面試的機會，雖然有時候我面試的表現並不好，這更是讓我深刻了解如果沒有學歷可能根本連面試的機會都沒有!

討論話題字彙

單字	音標	中譯
❶ academic	[ˌækəˋdɛmɪk]	學術的
❷ articulate	[ɑrˋtɪkjəˌlet]	闡釋
❸ obtain	[əbˋten]	獲得
❹ vocational	[voʊˈkeɪʃənl]	職業的
❺ candidate	[ˋkændədet]	候選人
❻ advantage	[ədˋvæntɪdʒ]	優點
❼ impress	[ɪmˈprɛs]	使…印象深刻
❽ realize	[ˋrɪəˌlaɪz]	了解

Tradition

傳統

Q1 Do you think wearing traditional costume is important?

MP3 052

你覺得穿傳統服裝很重要嗎？

I think it is important to keep the culture alive as much as possible, but a lot of traditions have become unpractical in the modern days. I think wearing traditional costume is one of the things that is disappearing fast because wearing a Chi-Pao is not fashionable, and not practical at all.

我覺得能夠盡量保持傳統是一件很重要的事，但是很多傳統到現在已經變得不合時宜。 我覺得穿傳統服裝是一件非常容易被淘汰的事，因為說真的穿旗袍真的沒有流行感，而且也非常不實穿。

I mean, how do you ride a scoot-

你看，如果穿旗

er when you are wearing a Chi-Pao? For that very reason, I think Vietnam has done a great job because their costume is actually practical, and it looks beautiful on the bike, too! That's why the traditional costume is still very popular in Vietnam.

袍你要怎麼騎機車呢？從這個觀點來看的話，我覺得越南的傳統服裝就很棒，因為不只實穿而且就騎車來看還更美！所以在越南穿傳統服裝的人還是很多。

I think if the designers can incorporate Chi-Pao with clothing of western design, it might make Chi-Pao more popular which might help us to keep the costume alive.

我覺得如果服裝設計師能夠把旗袍跟西式的服裝做結合，那旗袍的接受度會更高，這樣就更能延續傳統。

Q2 What are the traditions that you still practice at home? Why?

MP3 053

你們家有什麼傳統？為什麼要維持這個傳統？

One of the traditions is that we always stay up until midnight on Chinese New Year's eve and light fireworks with my dad. In the old days, people believe the sound of the fireworks scares the monster away, which is the reason why we celebrate Chinese New Year.

我家其中的一個傳統是，我們除夕的時候都會守夜到午夜，然後跟我爸爸一起放鞭炮。傳說鞭炮的聲音會把年獸嚇走，這也是我們慶祝新年的由來。

I love this tradition not because it is to do with Chinese New Year, but because we get to bond with my dad, and we are always so looking forward to doing it together. Another traditionis to do with birthdays, my mother insists to make us pig knuckle noodle soup for our birthday. It is a tradition she grew up with. It just

可是我喜歡這個傳統的原因並不是因為過年，而是可以跟我爸爸一起玩的回憶，我們總是既期待又興奮。另一個傳統是有關生日，我媽堅持我們生日一定要吃豬腳麵線，這是她從

reminds her with our grandma. 小到大的傳統，她總是會想起我的外婆。

討論話題字彙

單字	音標	中譯
❶ disappearing	[ˏdɪsəˋpɪrɪŋ]	消失的
❷ fashionable	[‘fæʃənəbl]	流行的
❸ practical	[‘præktɪkəl]	務實的
❹ incorporate	[ɪnˋkɔrpəˏret]	合併
❺ midnight	[ˋmɪdˏnaɪt]	午夜
❻ bond	[bɔnd]	產生連結
❼ forward	[‘fɔ:wəd]	向前
❽ remind	[rɪˋmaɪnd]	記起

Advertise-ment

廣告

Q1 In what way have advertisements changed in the past 10 years.

MP3 054

過去十年裡廣告有怎樣的轉變？

I think advertisements evolved rapidly over the past 10 years due to the popularity of the smartphone. It is almost impossible to avoid advertisements these days because they are literally everywhere.

我覺得廣告因為智慧型手機的普遍性，在過去十年裡轉變很大。現在幾乎睜開眼睛就可以看到廣告，因為真的到處都是。

In the old days, they were mostly on TV, magazines, and even on my scooter when I only walked away for

以前廣告大部分是在電視、雜誌或是機車上也有，就算我

a few hours! But nowadays, they are on my Facebook, LINE, and Wechat, they follow me wherever I go. Not only that, I think the presentation of the advertisement has become more technology orientated as well.

只不過離開幾個小時。反觀現在，臉書、LINE 或是微信上都有廣告。廣告好像追著我不放。不只這樣，我覺得呈現的方式也越來越高科技。

In order to draw viewers' attention, graphic designers use a lot of computer animation to make the advertisement stand out and make an impression on the viewer's mind. I think technology plays an important part in the advertisement evolution.

為了要引起觀眾的注意，視覺設計師會用很多電腦動畫來讓廣告引人注目，讓觀眾留下深刻印象。我覺得科技對廣告的轉變影響很大。

Q2 How do the advertisementsinfluence you on purchasing an item?

MP3 055

廣告對於你決定購買某樣物品時有怎樣的影響？

I think influence is not a big enough word, I would say advertisements actually brainwash the viewers and determine what they buy. I'd like to pay attention on the latest product and the easiest way is look at the advertisements, Some of the advertisements are very cleverly done, after I watched them, I actually felt the urge to rush out of the door to buy it and try it out!

我覺得用影響來形容還不夠貼切，應該要說廣告直接幫你洗腦而且控制你的選擇。我喜歡注意現在有什麼新產品，而最容易的方式就是看廣告，有些廣告拍得很好，我看了之後會很想衝出門去買那個產品來試試看！

Although sometimes the products I bought did not demonstrate the desired result, I felt deceived, but there is nothing I can do! The advertisement is feeding the information to me, and I was convinced,

雖然有時候有些產品實在是沒有廣告上講的神奇，我會覺得被騙，可是那也無可奈何。我只能說廣告知道我想聽什麼，

that's all I can say. 而且真的講到我的心坎裡。

討論話題字彙

單字	音標	中譯
❶ popularity	[ˌpɑːpjuˈlærəti]	流行
❷ literally	[ˋlɪtərəlɪ]	逐字地、照字面地
❸ presentation	[ˌprizɛnˋteʃən]	表現；描述
❹ animation	[ˌænəˋmeʃən]	卡通片、動畫片
❺ brainwash	[ˋbrenˏwɑʃ]	洗腦
❻ attention	[əˋtɛnʃən]	注意、注意力、專心
❼ cleverly	[ˋklɛvɚlɪ]	聰明地、靈巧地
❽ demonstrate	[ˋdɛmənˏstret]	論證、證明

05 Unit

Social media

社群網站

Q1 Do you think using social media poses danger in our lives?

MP3 056

你覺得使用社群網站對我們的生活有什麼潛在的危險嗎?

I think it is potentially dangerous because you have no idea who else has access to your profile other than your friends. What worries me the most is those people who like to update their location and activities in real time, it actually reveals more information than you think.

我覺得真的是有潛在的危險，因為你不知道除了你的朋友們，還有誰在看你的資料。其實最令人擔心的是那些喜歡即時上傳更新他們的所在地，還有從事的活動的人，這可是把你的行蹤都洩漏出去！

I know there is a privacy set-ting function, but not everybodyknows how it works.

我知道你可以更改隱私設定，可是不是每個人都知道怎麼改。

I was really surprised to find when someone shared your photo on Facebook, all his or her friends can see it, too. You just never know whether there is a predator out there waiting for his chance.

當我發現原來如果有人分享你的照片，你朋友的朋友們也都看的到，我很驚訝！你真不知道是不是有壞人在等待機會害你。

Q2 ▸ What do you think of people who do not use social media?

MP3 057

你對於不用社群網站的人有什麼感想？

I understand life is all about choices and social media might not be everyone's cup of tea. I do respect their choice, but honestly, people choosing not to use social media are likely to lose touch with most people in their lives. Almost everybody owns a smartphone nowadays, and people with smartphones tend to use social media to communicate instead of the conventional phone calls. Even my 70-year-old grandmother can use Skype to call me!

我了解生活中充滿的選擇而且不是每個人都喜歡用社群網站。我尊重他們的選擇可是說真的如果他們選擇不用社群網站，很可能他們會漸漸地跟周邊的人們失去聯絡，因為現在大家都有智慧型手機，而且大家反而不用傳統的方式打電話，都用社群網站在聯絡。連我七十歲的奶奶都會用Skype打電話給我！

I often wonder what is the reason that makes them resentful about

我總是在想是什麼原因讓人排斥使用

using social media and refuse to keep up with rest of the population. I guess they are not firm believers of selfies either; otherwise, I am sure they will be all over it.

社群網站而且情願跟其他人脱節。我覺得他們一定是不喜歡自拍，不然再多社群網站也不夠用！

討論話題字彙

單字	音標	中譯
❶ potentially	[pə`tɛnʃəlɪ]	潛在地、可能地
❷ access	[`æksɛs]	接近的機會、進入的權利、使用
❸ profile	[`profaɪl]	輪廓、外形、外觀
❹ reveal	[rɪ`vil]	揭示、揭露
❺ predator	[`prɛdətɚ]	食肉動物、掠奪者
❻ resentful	[rɪ`zɛntfəl]	忿恨的、怨恨的
❼ population	[ˌpɑpjə`leʃən]	人口
❽ selfie	[sɛlfi]	自拍照

present

禮物

Q1 How do you pick the perfect present for someone?

MP3 058

你是怎樣決定哪樣禮物最適合某個人？

I think first I will observe the person's lifestyle and see if there is anything that he or she might need or something that suits his or her lifestyle. Or I will try to have a conversation with the person and try to find out what he or she likes without giving too much away.

首先我會先觀察那個人的生活型態，再看看他是不是需要什麼東西，還是有某樣東西他生活中會用得上的。不然我會試著在不讓他知道的形況下，跟他聊聊他喜歡什麼東西。

If they seem to have everything they need, and I couldn't work out

如果他什麼都不缺的話，而且我也猜

what they want then I will organise a surprise instead, like taking them to a restaurant and prearrange with the restaurant for the staff to jump out and sing a song for him or something.

不出他要什麼的話，那我就會安排一個驚喜給他，就像先跟餐廳串通好，然後再帶他去餐廳，再請服務生出來幫他唱首歌之類的。

I think a memorable moment is the best gift that anyone can ask for! It doesn't have to be something tangible.

我覺得難忘的回憶就是最好的禮物，有錢也買不到！好的禮物不見得一定要是實體的東西。

Q 2

MP3 059

Are there special customs regarding giving and receiving presents in your country?

在你的國家有什麼送禮的習俗還是禁忌嗎？

Yes, there are. Most of the customs are based on the rhythm of the Chinese words which could sound like either bringing a good fortune or cursing to the person who receives the present. For Example, you would never give someone a wall clock as a present because it sounds like attending someone's funeral in Mandarin.

有的，大部分的習俗跟禁忌都是跟中文的押韻有關，不是聽起來像吉祥話，就是好像詛咒收禮物的人壞事會發生。舉個例子來說，你不能送時鐘給人當禮物，因為中文聽來很像是送終。

Another interesting one is, never give an umbrella to your partner because it sounds like you will be breaking up with him or her. Taiwanese believe if a pregnant woman handles sharp objects, such as nee-

另一個有趣的例子是不能送雨傘給男女朋友，因為有分手的意思。台灣人還相信孕婦不能碰尖的東西，像針還有剪刀之

dles and scissors it would cause miscarriage. I know this is purely based on superstitious reasons and there is no scientific evidence to prove it, but please do not buy a manicure set for your friend's baby shower.

類的，因為會害人流產。我知道這完全是迷信，一點科學根據都沒有，可是如果你朋友要辦孕媽媽寶寶臨盆前的派對，你千萬不要送她修指甲的剪刀組！

討論話題字彙

單字	音標	中譯
❶ observe	[əb`zɝv]	觀察、觀測
❷ conversation	[ˏkɑnvɚ`seʃən]	會話、談話
❸ memorable	[`mɛmərəb!]	值得懷念的
❹ tangible	[`tændʒəb!]	可觸知的、有實體的
❺ rhythm	[`rɪðəm]	節奏、韻律
❻ funeral	[`fjunərəl]	喪葬、葬儀
❼ superstitious	[ˏsupɚ`stɪʃəs]	迷信的
❽ evidence	[`ɛvədəns]	證據

Lifestyle

生活型態

Q1 Do you consider your lifestyle healthy?

MP3 060

你覺得你的生活型態健康嗎？

I think my lifestyle is relatively healthy because I like to look after my body, eat well, and exercise regularly. I try to stay away from junk food as much as I can, like fried chicken and burgers. I always make sure I eat enough fruits and vegetables as well. I think what I eat is not a concern, but I do have a very bad habit which is to stay up late at night.

我覺得我的生活型態還算健康啦！因為我還蠻注意飲食跟規律的運動。我是盡量不吃像炸雞或漢堡之類的垃圾食物。而且我蔬菜水果會吃足量。我覺得我最大的問題不是吃，而是我喜歡晚睡的壞習慣。

I find it very soothing to just sit there and watch TV alone at night.

我很喜歡晚上一個人坐在那裏看電視

Sometimes I struggle to turn off the TV and go to bed. By the time I look at the clock, it would be 12:30, or 1 am even. I get tired quite easily, so I can't really say my lifestyle is 100% healthy.

的感覺，很放鬆，放鬆到我有時候真的不想關電視去睡覺。等我抬頭看時間的時候，已經12點半了！有時候甚至已經1點了！我是蠻容易累的，所以我不能説我的生活型態百分百的健康。

Q 2 What do you think is better for you? Home cooking or eating out?

MP3 061

你覺得怎樣比較健康?在家吃還是出去吃?

Ever since food safety became an issue in Taiwan, I am deeply convinced that homecooking is much better for you than eating out. However, I still cannot guarantee that homecooking is 100 percent safer because we still don't know whether the ingredients we bought from the shops were produced properly, such as cooking oil.

自從食安問題在台灣延燒之後，我深深地相信家裡煮的東西是比外面的東西健康， 可是就算這樣説，我還是無法保證家裡的東西是安全無虞的，因為我們不知道我們買回來的原料是不是好的，例如煮飯用的油。但是比起外面的東西，至少我們還能控制我們自己煮到底加了什麼東西進去。

But I guess I have more control on what is actually in a dish if I cook

我可以保證絕對沒有防腐劑還有人工

at home. I know it definitely doesn't have any preservative or artificial flavouring in it. However, home cooking is still home cooking. It is not restaurant quality food. I would still eat out because the restaurant food just tastes so much better. I am willing to risk my health once in a while!

調味料。然而，家裡煮的東西也只是這樣而已，真的沒有外面餐廳的水準。所以我還是會出去吃因為餐廳的東西真的好吃很多，好吃到我情願拿健康來冒險！

討論話題字彙

單字	音標	中譯
❶ relatively	[`rɛlətɪvlɪ]	相對地
❷ regularly	[`rɛgjələ˞lɪ]	規律地
❸ struggle	[`strʌg!]	掙扎
❹ ingredient	[ɪn`gridɪənt]	成分
❺ properly	[`prɑpə˞lɪ]	適當地
❻ definitely	[`dɛfənɪtlɪ]	明顯地、清楚地
❼ preservative	[prɪ`zɝvətɪv]	防腐劑
❽ artificial	[ˌɑrtə`fɪʃəl]	人工的

Shopping

購物

Q1 Do you prefer to shop online or visit the stores?

MP3 062

你喜歡上網購物還是到實體店面去？

I actually like them both, but it depends how much time and how urgent I need the item. If I had a lot of time and was just trying to pick out something I want for a long time, I will browse online and compare the price and specification.

我其實兩個都喜歡，可是要看我有多少時間或是我急不急著要那個東西。如果我有很多時間可以只是想慢慢挑一個我喜歡的東西，那我會上網逛逛比較一下價格跟規格。

I know it will take a few days at least for it to be delivered, but I can wait because I am in no hurry.

我知道送來要等好幾天，可是無所謂我不急。

However, if I need to pick out something at the last minute, say I just realised it is a friend's birthday, and I need a present for him today, I will definitely go to the stores. I know I might pay more in the store, but it doesn't leave me with a choice really.

可是如果今天是臨時需要一個東西，就好像剛發現朋友生日，需要一個禮物，那我就會去店面裡買。我知道可能會貴一點但是我也沒辦法。

Q2 ▸ How do big supermarket chains affect the local traditional markets?

MP3 063

大型連鎖超市對當地的傳統市場有什麼影響？

I believe big supermarket chains would impact the profit of the local small business vendors, such as corner grocery store, local butcher, fish monger which is most of the stalls you found in a traditional market. I must say most of the younger generation are drawn to chain supermarkets because it is a one-stop shop, they are very well stocked with a wide range of varieties, you can even get make-up items there, and inside the store is bright and clean inside which is opposite to the traditional market.

我相信大型的連鎖超市絕對會影響傳統市場攤商的生意，尤其是像一般的雜貨店，賣肉的，賣魚的攤販。我必須要說，年輕一輩的都會被大型連鎖超市吸引，因為超市裡什麼都有賣，各式各樣的選擇很多，就連化妝品也有，而且店裡面明亮又乾淨，跟傳統市場完全相反。

Without the younger generation's

如果沒有年輕一

support of the local business, I think their business will really struggle especially when the younger generation start to take up the responsibility of cooking at home. The local market might not even exist by then.

輩的來支持傳統市場，我相信攤商的生意會很難做，尤其是等到年輕的這批人開始擔起家裡煮飯的責任，傳統市場可能也不存在了。

討論話題字彙

單字	音標	中譯
❶ urgent	[ˈɜ:rdʒənt]	緊急的
❷ browse	[braʊz]	瀏覽
❸ specification	[ˌspɛsəfɪˈkeʃən]	規格
❹ at least	[æt list]	至少
❺ vendor	[`vɛndɚ]	攤販
❻ monger	[`mʌŋgɚ]	販賣、製造
❼ drawn	[drɔn]	拉
❽ opposite	[`ɑpəzɪt]	相反的

Internet

網路

Q1 How does the Internet change the way that people have relationships with each other?

MP3 064

網路對人與人的交往有著什麼樣的影響和變化？

I don't know whether the internet has brought people closer or pushed us further apart because everything is just one click away, meeting or talking to people in person just seems like an idea of the past.

我不知道該說網路是讓人與人更靠近還是距離更遠，因為所有的事都可以上網處理。面對面的見面或聊天好像是過時的事。

I remember when I was younger I used to fight with my brother

我記得我小時候都跟我哥用 Face-through Facetime, and mind you, he was only upstairs in his bedroom!

time 吵架，可是其實他就在樓上的房間裡。

But by the same token, I never really felt he was far away when he moved out of home to pursue further studies. We chat all the time online. I found it very comforting to be able to see him while talking to him. I guess we are now accustomed to talking to a flat screen than a real person in front of you.

同樣的，當他因為讀書的原因搬出去的時候，我不覺得他離得很遠，因為我還是可以上網跟他見面聊天，讓我覺得有安心。我覺得大家應該很習慣對著平面的螢幕講話，反而不習慣跟人面對面聊天了。

Q2 Do you think meeting people online is a good thing?

MP3 065

你覺得上網交朋友是一件好事情嗎？

I don't see any harm in trying and honestly I think it is worth a shot especially when there is no other way to meet new people in the day-to-day routine. I know there are lots of dating sites or chat rooms where you can find people who are more like-minded or people who share common interests. I think all friendships have to start somewhere!

基本上我不覺得嘗試下有什麼不好的，因為如果每天固定的作息都沒辦法遇到其他人的話，那我覺得為什麼不試試看？我知道有很多交友網站或是聊天室可以加入，認識一些想法類似或是有共同興趣的人，友誼就是這樣開始的！

People seem to have this negative reaction when you told them you meet someone online. But I believe not everyone you meet online is there to get you. It is no different than meeting someone in a bar. You

可是大部分的人如果聽到你說你們是在網上認識的，都會有種負面的反應，可是我相信不是每個人都是壞人。這跟在酒

still need to practice your common sense and be aware of the stranger danger regardless of where you meet them.

吧認識人沒什麼兩樣，反正不管你們是在哪裡認識的，你還是要保持理智知道面對陌生人要小心。

討論話題字彙

單字	音標	中譯
❶ upstairs	[ˌʌpˈsterz]	樓上
❷ pursue	[pɚˋsu]	追求
❸ comforting	[ˈkʌmfɚtɪŋ]	舒適的
❹ accustomed	[əˋkʌstəmd]	適應的
❺ routine	[ruˋtin]	例行公事
❻ like-minded	[ˋlaɪkˋmaɪndɪd]	有志一同的
❼ common	[ˋkɑmən]	普遍的
❽ negative	[ˋnɛgətɪv]	負面的

Travel

旅遊

Q1 Do you prefer domestic travel or international travel?

MP3 066

你喜歡國內旅遊還是出國旅遊?

I would prefer international travel if I can afford it, because going to a foreign country is very exciting, especially going to an exotic country like Brazil or somewhere in the Middle East.

如果我負擔的起的話，我會比較喜歡出國旅行。到陌生的國家總是很有新鮮感尤其是那些異國風很濃的地方就像巴西或是某個中東國家。

The cultural and food are so different, just imagine you are in a carnival dancing with all the beautiful

特別是文化跟當地食物會很顯著的不同，想像一下你在巴

Brazilian girls or surrounded by the belly dancer while you are having lamb and flat bread.

西的嘉年華會跟那些美女一起跳舞，或是一邊享用著羊肉還有中東餅，桌邊被肚皮舞孃環繞著。

It would be a once-in-a-lifetime experience! It is not something that you can experience in Taiwan. I would love to support domestic tourism more as well, but Taiwan is a small country, I think I have pretty much been to most of the tourist attractions anyway. It is just not as exciting as going overseas.

那些是一生難得的回憶，是在台灣感受不到的體驗。我也想支持國內旅遊可是台灣是個小國家，我覺得我好像大部分的觀光勝地我都去過了，真的沒什麼新鮮感了。

Q2 Do you prefer joining the pre-organised tour group or self-guided tour?

MP3 067

你比較喜歡跟團旅遊還是自由行？

I actually like the combination of both. I like to explore a new place at my own pace and interests. I will do my research prior to departure to work out a plan on what I would like to see and do once I get there. I will also research methods of transportation from point A to point B.

我其實喜歡混搭。我去旅遊的時候我喜歡照自己的意思走。我在出發之前會先做好功課，決定我到了當地之後想做什麼。我同時也會研究一下從A處到B處的交通方式。

If I get enough information and am confident about getting there on my own, I will go fully self-guided. However, in some places I will prefer to join the local tour because sometimes it works out more economically and other time it is just much easier in terms of transportation, especially

如果我的資訊很充足，而且沒有什麼問題的話，那我就會完全自己走。可是有些地方我是會比較想參加當地旅行團的，因為有時候其實參加旅行團比較便宜，不

those areas where there is no direct road to get there.

然就是交通上方便多了，尤其是想去那些很難自己可以去得到的地方。

討論話題字彙

單字	音標	中譯
❶ carnival	[`kɑrnəv!]	嘉年華
❷ surrounded	[sə`raʊnd]	環繞的
❸ attractions	[ə`trækʃəns]	吸引力
❹ overseas	[`ovɚ`siz]	海外的
❺ combination	[ˏkɑmbə`neʃən]	結合
❻ departure	[dɪ`pɑrtʃɚ]	出發、起程
❼ self-guided	[`sɛlf`gaɪdɪd]	自動導向的
❽ economical	[ˏikə`nɑmɪk!]	節約的

Technology

科技

Q1 Do you think people are spending too much time looking at their phones nowadays?

MP3 068

你覺得現代人是不是花太多時間在看手機?

It is a definite yes from me. I think I am guilty as charged. I find it hard to put my phone down, and I am constantly checking my phone to see if there is a message from someone. I must say I do get a bit sad if I don't hear from my friends for too long. It almost seems I am addicted to my cell phone ! But the thing is, I know I am not alone, and most people are like me these days.

沒錯，我就是這樣！我有時候真的沒辦法把電話放下來不看，而且我會一直拿出來看是不是有人傳訊息給我，我沒接到。我承認如果我朋友太久沒有傳訊息給我的話，我還會有點失落感，可以說我幾乎手機上癮了。可是，我絕對不是唯一一個，大部分的人都跟我一樣啊！

The phone is not only a phone anymore, it is so versatile which can transform into anything. You can check your email, you can use it as a GPS, you can shop online.You name it!

手機已經不再只是手機了，隨時隨地都可以變成你想要的東西。你可以查你的電子郵件，你可以用它來當導航系統，還可以上網購物。你想得出來它就做得到！

Q2 How does technology help our lives?

MP3 069

科技對我們的生活有什麼幫助?

I think technology definitely makes our lives much easier or maybe I should say it probably made us lazier because it brought a lot of convenience to our lives. We take so much for granted compared with our parents' generation. I remember my mother was telling me she had to go and collect fire wood for the wood stove, so my grandmother could cook in the kitchen.

我覺得科技的進步讓我們的生活容易很多，或是我應該説科技進步讓我們變得很懶惰因為它帶來了很多的方便性。比起我父母的年代，我們真的太不知道感恩。我記得有一次我媽跟我説她小時候需要去撿柴回家在灶裡生火，這樣我外婆才可以在廚房煮飯。

I guess we are the lucky generation, we grew up with a lot of technology already in place such as telephone, TV, gas stove and microwaves. I am happy about how technology has advanced. I cannot picture

所以我覺得我們真的是很幸福的一代，我們從小就對科技不陌生有電話、電視、瓦斯爐還有微波爐。我很慶幸有跟上

myself going and finding firewood to collect! I don't think I would survive in that era.

科技進步的速度，我無法想像還要去撿柴的生活，我覺得我在那個年代應該活不下去。

討論話題字彙

單字	音標	中譯
❶ constantly	[ˋkɑnstəntlɪ]	不斷地
❷ addicted	[əˋdɪktɪd]	上癮的
❸ versatile	[ˈvɚsətəl, -ˌtaɪl]	多才多藝的
❹ transfer	[trænsˋfɝ]	轉移
❺ granted	[ˋgræntɪd]	獲准
❻ generation	[ˌdʒɛnəˋreʃən]	世代
❼ advanced	[ædˈvænst]	進階的
❽ survive	[sɚˋvaɪv]	存活

Part 4

最後衝刺試題

· **精益求精**：除了基礎 3 個 part 的核心官方必考話題，額外包含 61 題強力考前衝刺題，累積關鍵實力、舉一反三，應試即獲取高分。

· 強力衝刺話題均涵蓋了在 3 個 part 中都可能考到的考點，其他考題均無出其右，能使考生受用不淺，於應試時即使不及細想亦能答得恰到好處，獲取考官青睞。

一問三答 MP3 070

01 Question

What's your favorite waterfall? Why?

你最喜歡的瀑布是哪一個？為什麼呢？

Niagara Falls is my favorite waterfall. The falls are big, beautiful and very loud. And you get to travel to New York and Canada since it's right in the middle of the two places. At night time the falls are even lighted up with colorful lights. I'm definitely going there for my honeymoon. It's just very romantic in general.

尼加拉瀑布是我最喜歡的瀑布。那裡的瀑布又大又美，而且瀑布聲響亮。而且你還可以順便去紐約或是加拿大旅行，因為它剛好在兩個地方的中間。在晚上的時候他們還會有色彩繽紛的燈亮起。我一定要去那裡度蜜月。整體來說那就是一個很浪漫的地方啊。

My favorite one is Victoria Falls in Africa. It's one of the Seven Natural Wonders of the world, and it's so easy to see once you're there. The hardest part is to get there I guess. It is one of the largest and most inspiring in the world. The waterfall is about 108 meters long. I am still in awe of it.

我最喜歡的是在非洲的維多利亞瀑布。那是世界七大奇景之一，而且一旦你到了那裡之後你就會很輕易地知道為什麼它是七大奇景之一。我想最難的地方就是要先到非洲吧。那是世界上最大也是最激勵人心的瀑布之一。整個瀑布大概有一百八十公尺長。我到現在還是覺得很驚人 。

I really like the Rainbow Falls at Big Island, Hawaii. Just like its name suggests, the rainbow can be seen every sunny morning at around 10 am. The waterfall flows over a natural lava cave, which was believed to be one of the Hawaiian goddess's home. How romantic is that?

我真的很喜歡在夏威夷大島的彩虹瀑布。就像它的名字一樣，每個晴天的早上十點左右都可以看到彩虹。瀑布是從天然的火山岩洞穴傾流而下，那個洞穴也聽說是夏威夷一個女神的家。真的超浪漫的！

一問三答 MP3 071

02 Question

What do you usually like to do at the waterfalls?

你通常都喜歡在瀑布做什麼呢？

I usually try to find the best angle to take a picture with the waterfall. That's all it's about for me really. I finally make it that far to the waterfall, and all I really want is to have a decent picture with the waterfall. It's a good incentive to hike to the waterfall for me.

我通常都會試著找跟瀑布照相最好的角度。對我來說那是最重要的。我好不容易才到了瀑布，而且我真正最想要的只是一張跟瀑布的漂亮合照。對我來說那是健行到瀑布很好的動力。

There are so many things you can do at the waterfall. My friends and I like to jump off the rock and swim. When the water is clean, it is the most refreshing feeling you get. We usually do cannon ball or just dive under the waterfall. Of Course, we only jump off when it is safe at that place.

在瀑布有很多事情可以做啊。我的朋友跟我都很喜歡從石頭上跳下去游泳。當水很乾淨的時候，那是最令人覺得清新的感覺。我們通常都會抱膝跳水製造很大的水花或是潛到瀑布底下。當然那是在安全的狀況之下我們才會跳水啦。

I usually hike to the waterfall, and swim around when it's safe. Or I would take a step back and just try to take everything in. Sometimes I like to meditate on the rock while listening to the waterfall. It's like one of those nature sounds CDs only it's real there.

我通常會健行到瀑布，然後安全的話還會到處游游。或者我會退一步，然後就把那美景盡收眼底。有的時候我也喜歡聽著瀑布的聲音然後坐在岩石上面打坐。那就好像是在聽那些大自然的聲音 CD 一樣。

一問三答 MP3 072

03 Question What do you love or hate about waterfalls?
你喜歡或是不喜歡瀑布的哪裡呢？

Michelle 蜜雪兒

I love how beautiful the waterfalls are naturally, but I really hate how dangerous the hike can be sometimes. The hike is usually wet and muddy. A lot of slipping and sliding skills are required. Often a lot of accidents happen each year. I don't understand why no more security measures are in play.

我當然很喜歡瀑布有多麼的漂亮，但是有的時候我也真的很討厭去瀑布的步道因為其危險性。那個步道通常都是很濕又泥濘。存著許多打滑處因此會需要用到滑來滑去的技能。而且每年也都有很多意外會發生。我真的不懂為什麼沒有更多的安全措施。

Matt 麥特

It's just amazing to see what nature can offer. The huge body of water happens to fall with the perfectly vertical rock, creating one of the most beautiful sceneries in the world. Who would have thought that we are so easy to entertain? God must be a pretty smart parent...

就真的很神奇可以看到大自然製造出來的東西。這麼多的水剛好隨著那垂直的石頭落下，創造出來世界上最漂亮的美景之一。誰想得到我們會那麼好娛樂？神一定是一個很聰明的父母親...。

Besides the fact that it's usually free, waterfalls are actually very beneficial for our bodies. The moving water results in negative ions. Somehow these negative ions result in increased serotonin levels in our brain, which makes us more relaxed and happier. Natural remedy for a stressed office lady right there!

除了它通常都是免費的之外，瀑布也有很多對我們身體很有益處的地方。流動的水製造了負離子，然後這些負離子就使得我們頭腦裡的血清激素增高，因為那樣我們就會覺得更加放鬆，或是更開心。那就是大自然對壓力很大的上班族的天然療癒啊！

一問三答 MP3 073

04 Question

What are your impressions of a lake?

你對湖的印象是什麼？

Beautiful but boring. My cousin's family has a property by the lake in New Zealand. We visit them from time to time, but I just don't know what to do rather than sitting by the lake and get tanned. At first, I was impressed with the beautiful scenery, but then I thought to myself: "I would spend my money on somewhere else." I feel like I automatically get old when I'm by the lake. You know what I mean?

美麗但是很無聊。我表姐他們家在紐西蘭的湖邊有棟房子。我們有時候會拜訪他們，可是我真的不知道除了坐在湖邊曬太陽之外還可以做什麼。一開始的時候我對那裡的美景很驚艷，可是後來我跟自己說：「我會把錢花在別的地方」。每次我在湖邊的時候我就覺得我好像自動老了好幾歲。你懂嗎？

Campfire, fishing, and refreshing morning swims. I think it would be so awesome to just stay a few days or weeks by the lake. I was in the

Boy Scout growing up, and we would spend our summer by the lake and learn how to fish and camp. The memory by the lake is definitely one of my favorite childhood memories. The buddy I met there is still one of my best friends.

營火、釣魚，還有清涼的晨泳。我覺得如果可以在湖邊待上個幾天或是幾個禮拜一定會超棒的。我小時候有加入童子軍，暑假的時候我們會在湖邊學怎麼釣魚還有露營。我最喜歡的兒時回憶之一就是暑假在湖邊的時光。我在那邊認識的一個朋友現在還是我最好的朋友之一。

Lakes always give me an impression of calmness. I try to think about lakes when I'm really angry sometimes. It sounds funny but it really works. When I'm very stressed about work, I'll try to think about lakes and it always brings me peace. I actually put a poster of a lake with the caption "Keep Calm and Carry On" in front of my office desk.

湖總是給我一個很平靜的印象。有時候我很生氣的時候我就會試著想著湖。聽起來很好笑可是真的很有用。我如果工作壓力很大的時候我就會想像著湖泊，然後我就會平靜一些。其實我有在我辦公桌前貼了一張湖泊的海報，上面寫著：「保持冷靜，繼續前進。」

一問三答 MP3 074

05 Question

Which lake do you want to visit? Why?

你最想要去哪一個湖？為什麼？

Lake Louise! I saw it on the magazine randomly and I was very impressed with the hotel there. I heard it costs a fortune to stay there for a night, but I guess it's worth the money. I tried to call the travel agency about one of their tour packages there, but it's all booked out. I've already made a reservation for next summer though. It's one of the most fancy hotels, so I have to see it myself.

露易絲湖！我有一次不小心在雜誌上看到就對那裡的飯店印象深刻。聽說在那住一晚超級貴，但我想應該是值得的。我有試著打給旅行社問他們那裡其中一個行程，可是全部都訂光了。但我有立刻下訂明年暑假去那裡的行程。那飯店是最豪華的飯店之一，我一定要親自瞧瞧。

I've always wanted to go to the Loch Ness in Scotland. You know how it is! All those myths and legends you hear growing up. They just always fascinate me. When I first knew about Nessie, unlike everybody else, I was not surprised at all. I've always believed that there are some kinds of monsters in the lakes.

我一直都很想要去在蘇格蘭的尼斯湖。你懂得！從小聽說了那麼多關於它的神話和傳說。我總是對它很好奇。當我第一次聽到 Nessie 的時候，我沒有像其他人那麼驚訝。我一直都覺得在湖裡一定住著某種怪物。

I heard about the Jellyfish Lake in Palau, and it got me really curious. It's pretty much a lake full of jellyfish. Sounds scary, but miraculously all the jellyfish aren't poisonous at all. Long story short, the jellyfish were originally from the ocean but the land rose, so the jellyfish was trapped in the lake. Overtime, they lost their predators, so there was no reason for them to be poisonous anymore. People can jump in the lake and swim with them without getting harmed. Palau is relatively cheaper to travel and their official language is English. Perfect.

我聽說過在帛琉的水母湖然後就一直對它很好奇。它其實就是一個充滿了水母的湖。聽起來很恐怖，可神奇的是在那裡所有的水母都沒有毒。長話短說就是本來那些水母來自海洋，直到有天陸地上升，所以那些水母就被困在湖泊裡。隨著時間過去，水母們失去了牠們的天敵，而也就沒有需要毒素的必要。人可以跳到湖裡跟牠們游泳也不會受傷。帛琉相對之下也是一個旅行比較便宜的地方，而且他們的官方語言是英文，太完美了。

一問三答 MP3 075

06 Question

Do you prefer to swim in the lake or in the ocean?

你比較想要在湖裡還是海裡游泳？

Oh, I don't swim. I mean, I can swim, but I don't really swim. If swimming were only for the exercise, why would I swim in the lake or ocean while there are swimming pools and gyms? Who knows what's in the ocean and lakes.

喔，我不游泳。我的意思是說，我會游泳，但我平常不會真的去游。如果游泳只是為了運動，有泳池和健身房，我幹嘛要去湖裡或是海裡游泳？誰知道在海裡還有湖裡有什麼。

As much as I love the lakes, I prefer to swim in the ocean. There is something about the combination of the sun and ocean. It always makes me so happy after I jump in the salty water. It's an instant stress relief for me.

儘管我很喜歡湖，我還是比較喜歡在海裡游泳。海和陽光有種令人無法解釋的元素。每次我跳入鹹鹹的海水之後總是很開心。對我來說那是一個即時減壓的辦法。

I prefer swimming in the lake. It's just calm water, so I don't have to worry about either the currents or the waves. It allows total relaxation. Better yet, you don't feel all sticky after swimming in the lake!

我比較喜歡在湖裡游泳。因為湖水很平靜，所以我不用擔心急流或是海浪。在湖裡游泳我才能真正的放鬆。更棒的是，在湖裡游泳以後也不會全身黏黏的。

一問三答 MP3 076

07 Question

What are some of the most interesting caves in the world?

世界上有哪一些有趣的洞穴呢？

Have you heard about the Cave of Crystals in Mexico? Doesn't it just sound so fascinating? I randomly read about it in a magazine, while I was getting a haircut, and I have been really interested about going to see it. It's said that the crystal formation in that cave is huge. It is over 9 meters long and 1 meter wide. I really want to see this giant crystal, but I heard it's disturbingly hot in that cave. Well...no wonder the crystal is still there...

你有聽過墨西哥的巨型水晶洞穴嗎？你不覺得聽起來就很吸引人嗎？我有一次在剪頭髮的時候無意間在雜誌上看到的，然後我就一直想去看。聽說在洞穴裡的水晶體十分巨大。大概有九公尺高，然後一公尺寬。我是真的很想去看這個巨型水晶，但是我聽說在洞穴裡是超級熱的。哎…難怪那些水晶都還在那…

There is an interesting cave in the island of Capri in Italy. It's interesting because there's an eerie blue light in the cave. I went to that cave in the afternoon, which was a really good time to visit because that was the time when the sunlight was filtered through seawater and created a blue reflection. It was phenomenal to see. I took so many pictures there.

在義大利卡布里島有一個很有趣的洞穴。它很有趣是因為它洞穴裡有一道很詭異的藍光。我去的時候是在下午，聽說那是一個很好的時機，因為那時候陽光會透過海水照進洞穴，然後就會產生反射的藍光。真的是很壯觀。我在那拍了超多照片的。

When I was doing a Working Holiday in New Zealand, I went to Aranui cave that is known for its glowworms. Glowworms are very much like fireflies but they are different from each other. It's a must see in that area. When I went in the cave on a boat ride, there were thousands of glowworms illuminating. That was the most beautiful scene I've ever seen.

我在紐西蘭度假打工的時候有去一個以螢火蟲聞名的阿拉努伊洞穴。在洞穴裡的這種螢火蟲跟一般的螢火蟲不太一樣。在那個區域是必看的。我坐船去那個洞穴看的時候，那裡有上千隻螢火蟲在發光。那是我目前為止看過最美的景象。

一問三答 MP3 077

08 Question

What kind of equipment do you think you need to explore caves?

你覺得探索洞穴的時候需要哪一些配備呢？

Speaking from my past experience, I definitely need to bring clothes that I don't care about. It is just so wet and muddy in the caves. I ruined a white T-shirt and my brand name shoes the last time I was in a cave. I was very upset. So, boots and towels to dry off as well. I don't have to be a cavewoman when I go to a cave, right?

這是我的經驗談，我一定要帶我不在意的衣服。因為洞穴裡真的又濕又泥濘。我有一次去洞穴裡的時候就毀了我一件白色Ｔ恤和一雙名牌的鞋子。我那時候真的很不爽。所以囉，靴子還有要擦乾的毛巾。我去洞穴不代表我就要變成一個野蠻人對吧？

I've heard a lot of stories when people got stuck in the caves. So, I think for me, I would want to bring extra food and water. Ropes and warm clothes to prepare for the worst. I might sound paranoid, but better safe than sorry, right?

我有聽過很多人被困在洞穴裡的故事。所以我想對我來說，我會要帶多點的食物和水，繩子還有保暖的衣服來作最壞的打算。我聽起來好像有點神經質，可是安全一點總比之後遺憾還要好吧？

Of course you need to bring a helmet, flashlight, and extra lights actually just in case. A raincoat would come in handy when you go exploring the caves. You have to watch out for some cave creatures, so you might want to bring company. It can be kind of creepy walking in caves.

當然你會需要安全帽、手電筒，還有額外的燈以防萬一。有雨衣的話，在你去探索洞穴的時候也是很方便的。還要小心一些洞穴裡的生物，所以帶個夥伴也是一個好主意。走在洞穴裡的時候其實還蠻令人毛骨悚然的。

一問三答 MP3 078

09 Question

What are some of the stories you have heard about caves?

你有聽過關於洞穴的什麼故事嗎？

Michelle 蜜雪兒

I saw the animation called The Croods a while back. It was a really cute story. The Croods are the last group of cavemen on earth, and they believe that they cannot leave the cave once it's dark. It's their only safe place when the darkness comes until one day they started their adventure outside of the cave and pursued the sun. It's a really funny and sweet story.

我前陣子有看了一部動畫叫做古魯家族。那是一個很可愛的故事。古魯家族是世界上唯一剩下的野人。他們相信他們天黑之後就一定不能離開洞穴。天黑之後他們唯一安全的地方就是洞穴裡。直到有一天他們開始了在洞穴外面追逐著太陽的冒險。那是一個很好笑又很窩心的電影 。

Matt 麥特

The only thing I can think of is Bat Man. The cave is where Bat Man stores all his undercover life. That's always my favorite part when the Bat Man drives his car out of the cave, and the bats fly out with him.

我唯一想到的就是蝙蝠俠。蝙蝠俠就是在洞穴裡面儲藏他所有的臥底生活。我最喜歡的一部分就是當蝙蝠俠開車飛出洞穴的時候，很多蝙蝠跟著他飛起的那幕。

Everyone knows about Plato's allegory of the cave! A bunch of people grew up in a cave, and when one of them got out of the cave, he had a hard time getting used to the sunlight, but then he saw the beauty of the world, and decided to go back and told his people about it. Everyone thought he was crazy and killed him. It's crazy what people would do to stay in their comfort zone.

大家都知道柏拉圖的洞穴的寓言。有一群人是在洞穴裡面長大的，然後當他們其中一個人走出了洞穴，他很難適應陽光，但是當他適應了之後，他看見了這個世界有多美，他決定會回去告訴其他人。但是大家都以為他瘋了要帶他們出洞穴，於是他們就把他殺了。大家為了要待在舒適圈裡而做出來的事真的是很誇張。

一問三答 MP3 079

10 Question Have you ever been to any National parks? If not, which one do you want to visit? 你有去過國家公園嗎？沒有的話，你想要去哪一個國家公園呢？

Michelle 蜜雪兒

I've been to several National parks in the world, but I would tell you that Jiuahaigou Vally National Park in China is just magical. The five-colored lakes, the clear sky and the evergreen forests are just amazing on its own. Heaven on earth would be the best description for it.

我有去過全世界很多座國家公園，但是我覺得最夢幻的是中國的九寨溝國家公園。五色沼、晴朗的天空和常青的森林分開看就已經很美了。對它最好的描述就是人間天堂。

Matt 麥特

I've been to Arenal National Park in Costa Rica. I heard many movies were shot in that National park. I have no doubts about it. It's just so lush and there is an active volcano within the national park! How cool is that! Because of the volcano, there are plenty of hot springs as well. If you talk to the locals, they will take you to the hidden waterfalls, too!

我有去過哥斯大黎加的 Arenal 國家公園。我聽說很多電影在那裡拍攝過。我完全沒有疑問。那裡真的很翠綠，而且還有一個活火山在國家公園裡。超酷的！因為有火山，那裡也有很多的溫泉。如果你跟當地人聊天認識的話，他們還會帶你去秘密瀑布呢！

Yes, I've been to Yosemite National Park. The view there is just breathtaking. I went in spring and that was when all the wildflowers were in bloom. Besides, the crystalline lakes and the pine forests just make perfect postcard-worthy views all around you!

有啊，我有去過優勝美地國家公園。那裡的景色真的美不勝收。我是春天的時候去的，在那個時候所有的野花都盛開。除此之外，清澈的湖水和松樹森林讓你周遭的景色都好像明信片一樣。

一問三答 MP3 080

11 Question

What are the things you expect to see or do in the National Parks?

你預期在國家公園可以看到什麼或是做什麼呢？

Michelle 蜜雪兒

I expect to join the guided tour in the National Parks. I cannot stress enough the importance of letting people who know what they are doing show you around in their playground. Horseback riding tours, or some private tours would be ideal.

我預期可以參加國家公園裡的導覽。我沒辦法強調讓知道該做什麼的人帶你去他們的地盤參觀的重要性。騎馬行程，或是一些私人行程都很理想。

Matt 麥特

I expect to see a lot of wildlife in the National Parks for sure. Some National Parks even give out maps of where to see those animals. Bear, bighorn sheep, bison, elk, and river otters all wander in the parks. I was once really close to a bear. It was frightening, but also amazing to see a bear in such a short distance. I was in awe to see such a beautiful creature in the National Parks and I would love to see more of them.

我一定是預期在國家公園裡看到很多野生動物。有一些國家公園甚至會給你一個地圖去看動物。熊、大角羊、美洲野牛、麋鹿和水獺都在公園裡到處遊蕩。我有一次很接近一隻熊。其實蠻恐怖的，但是同時也是很神奇可以這麼近看著熊。我那時候看到這麼美的生物真的很震撼，我還想要再看多一些。

I've always imagined the stars are all over the place in the National Parks, the forests and all that jazz. Avatar is what I have in mind when it comes to the National Parks. I also want to do some hiking and camping when I'm in a National Park I think.

我總是想像在國家公園裡到處都是星星、森林諸如此類的。想到國家公園我就會想到阿凡達。我也想要在國家公園裡健行或是露營。

一問三答 MP3 081

12 Question

What do you think is the purpose of the National Parks?
你覺得國家公園的目的是什麼？

Off the record, I think the real purpose of the National Parks is to attract more tourists and make money out of it. Think about it, the land has always been there, and the government claims the land and builds a park on it. What is the difference between a National Park and an entertainment park?

私下跟你說，我覺得國家公園真正的目的只是要吸引遊客來賺多一點錢。你想想看，土地本來就在那裡，國家徵收那個土地，然後在上面蓋了個公園。那國家公園跟遊樂園之間有什麼不一樣？

I was volunteering at the Yellowstone National Park for a while. The purpose of the National Park is to preserve and protect the natural resources for the future generation. We really do a lot to help preserve the beauty of the park. Places like that should be well preserved so that more people can see them in the future.

我有在黃石國家公園當了一陣子的志工。國家公園的目的是在於為了下一代保存，還有保護國家資源。我們在園區內真的做了很多保護美景的工作。這麼美麗的地方應該要被好好的保存下來給未來更多的人看到。

I think besides the obvious reason to preserve the place, most National Parks are trying to educate people about the place. They often provide opportunities for people to experience and understand the wildlife and the environment. I think it's a classroom where the real education happens.

我想除了很明顯的保存那個地方之外，大多數的國家公園也都試著要宣導那個國家公園。他們也會有讓人們體驗或瞭解野生動物或是環境的機會。我覺得國家公園是一個教育真的發生的教室。

一問三答 MP3 082

13 Question Have you ever been to any canyon?
你有曾經去過任何峽谷嗎？

Canyon? Me? No way! Do you know how many accidents happened at the canyons? People fall in there all the time. Alright, I might be a little dramatic, but you get the point. And who knows, what if it rains, there might be falling rocks! I certainly do not want to wear helmets when I'm traveling. I travel with styles. Period.

峽谷？我嗎？不可能的！你知道在峽谷有多少意外發生過嗎？大家一天到晚都掉到峽谷裡。好啦，我是有點誇張，可是你知道我的意思。而且誰知道啊，如果下雨的話，還可能會有落石耶！我真的不想要戴安全帽旅行。我要很時尚的旅行。就是這樣。

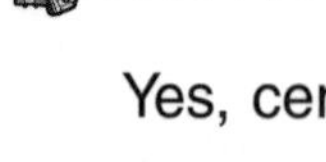

Yes, certainly. That's one of the must-sees for me. I went to Grand Canyon a few years ago, and it didn't disappoint me in any way! It was just as grand as I imagined. I feel so teeny when I was there. It's definitely a place that humbles you. The Native Americans consider this place as a holy place, and I can see that.

有啊，當然。那是我必去的地方之一。我幾年前有去過大峽谷，而且他也完全沒有令我失望！那就跟我想像的一樣那麼大！我在那裡的時候覺得我好小喔。那個地方真的會讓你覺得很謙卑。那裡同時也是印第安人覺得是很神聖的地方，我看得出來。

I was traveling in Tibet, and had a chance to visit the Yurlung Tsangpo Canyon. They claimed that it was the highest river in the world, and that's why the name of the canyon meant “The Everest of Rivers”. It is a place that's really close to heaven I think. Very pure and clean.

我有去西藏玩然後去了雅魯藏波峽谷。他們號稱那裡是世界上最高的河流。那也是它名字的意思。意思是說那是河流裡的聖母峰。而且我也覺得那裡是最接近天堂的地方。非常的純淨跟乾淨。

一問三答 *MP3 083*

14 Question Why do you think canyons are so popular?
你覺得為什麼峽谷很受歡迎呢？

Honestly I have no clue. I guess people would say something about the wonder of the nature blah-blah-blah, but what about safety? What happens to treasuring your own precious life? Many people went missing in the canyons, and I can imagine where they went.

老實說我真的不懂耶。我想大家可能會說因為那是大自然的奇景啊這類無聊的話，但是安全怎麼辦？要怎麼保護我們寶貴的生命呢？很多人在峽谷裡失蹤，我可以想像他們是去了哪裡。

I don't know. I like it because it's just a great reminder to stay humble, and it's only natural to be drawn to something so grand. Not to mention that none of it is manmade. It's all from our mother earth. We only live at small parts on this planet, and I can't wait and I know for sure that more wonders will be discovered in the future.

我不知道耶。我喜歡是因為那是可以提醒我保持謙卑的地方，而且我覺得是很自然而然被這麼巨大的地方吸引。更別提它完全不是人造的。完全是來自我們的大地之母。我們只住在這個星球上很小的一部分，我等不及要看，而且我確定有更多的奇景在這個世界上等著被探索。

Well...it's mostly because we heard these places during geography class when we were growing up. You know the name, and then you start watching Discovery or National Geographic channel. It's one of the most amazing things, and it must be true because textbooks and Discovery and National Geographic don't lie. The next thing you know, you're posting a picture on Facebook of you and the canyon.

嗯…我想大多是因為我們以前在上地理課的時候就有聽過這些地方，你就知道那些名字。然後你就開始看探索或是國家地理頻道。那是世界上最驚人的事物之一，而且也一定是真的，因為課本、探索，還有國家地理頻道不會騙人。然後你就發現你正在臉書上 po 一張你跟峽谷的照片。

一問三答 MP3 084

15 Question

Where have you seen the most beautiful sunrise?

你在哪裡看過最美的日出？

Sunrise? Of course at Mountain Ali in Taiwan! Where else do you go? When I was there, I had to lower myself to everyone's level to get in the tiny train for getting up to the mountain. I'd always imagined that we'd get in a luxurious chariot at 3 or 4 in the morning and just wave around the sparklers. So dreamy, and then some servers would have delicious food ready on the side when you are enjoying the sunrise. I guess they didn't live up to my expectation at all!

看曙光？當然是要去阿里山啊？不然你覺得還有什麼地方好去？想當初我去看的時候可是勉強搭乘小火車上去？我一直覺得該乘坐豪華馬車零晨三四點左右，邊拿著仙女棒朝著天空劃呀劃的。蠻夢幻的。然後隨從們還準備好美食，在看曙光時享用。我想他們一點也沒有我預期的那麼好。

I went to Haleakala in the Island of Maui. My friends and I got up at

3 so that the traffic to the mountain wasn't too bad. We made it to the top, and quickly found out it was freezing there. Luckily we brought a lot of extra blankets in the car. When the sun was about to rise, the colors of the cloud changed so quickly that I had no choice but to keep taking a lot of pictures. When the sun rose, everyone was in awe of the scene in front of us.

我去茂伊島的哈來阿卡拉。我的朋友跟我三點就起床了所以比較不會塞車。我們登頂的時候很快就發現山上超冷的。好險我們車子裡有多帶一些毯子。當太陽快要升起的時候，雲的顏色變化無窮所以我只好一直拍。當太陽真的升起的時候，大家都對眼前的景色感到震驚。

I watched the sunrise at Fiji. It was during the New Year's Eve actually. My friends and I decided that we wanted to catch one of the first sunrises in the world to welcome the upcoming New Year, so we went to Fiji and it was very nice. We completed our first of the year by scuba diving afterwards as well!

我在斐濟看日出。那時候其實是跨年夜。我的朋友和我想要看到世界上最早出來的日出來歡迎新的一年，所以我們就去斐濟，然後也真的蠻棒的。我們看完日落之後就去深潛來讓這新年的第一天更完美。

一問三答 MP3 085

16 Question

What are some most important things to bring when you go camping?

哪些重要的東西是你露營的時候會帶的？

Bug repellent is definitely one of the most important things I'll bring. I only use the ones with natural ingredients since I have sensitive skin. I'm born to attract all kinds of bugs. They will eat me alive in the wild. A scar is probably the one souvenir I don't want from the trip. Also, sunscreen is a must when I'm outdoors. Who wants to travel with sunburnt? Not this girl! Oh, and my feather pillow to ensure a good night sleep.

驅蟲液一定是我會帶的東西之一。我只用天然成分的驅蟲液因為我是敏感肌膚。我生下來就是會吸引各種的昆蟲。在野外他們會把我生吞掉。旅行的時候我唯一不想帶回來的紀念品就是疤痕。還有，如果我在戶外的話，防曬乳也是一定要的。誰想要邊旅行邊曬傷？不會是我！噢還有我的羽絨枕頭，確保我晚上睡得很好。

A water bottle and iodine are always good to have when you need to track down the water source. I bring my fishing pole with me whenever I'm going to be close to the water. It's good to kill time, and you might catch nutritional dinner. You never know! Most importantly, an open mind is always good since you never know who you are going to run into. I love to talk to people and listen to their stories. An open mind usually leads me to the most amazing experiences.

如果你需要找水源的話，有水壺和碘在身邊的話是很好的。如果我知道我會在水邊露營的話，我也都會帶我的釣竿。那很好殺時間而且說不定你有可能會抓到你的營養晚餐。最重要的是，一個開放的心胸，因為你永遠不知道你會遇到誰。我很喜歡很別人聊天，和聽他們的故事。一個開放的心胸總是帶給我很美好的經驗。

I have this lantern with solar battery. It's called Luci. It's pretty fantastic. It's light, and lasts for a long time. The bottom line is that the price is so reasonable as well. Also, a spork usually comes in handy when you're eating. A GPS, a simple first aid kit... You can never be over prepared.

我有一個太陽能電池的提燈。它叫 Luci。它超棒的。很輕又可以持續很久的時間。最重要的是它的價錢也很合理。還有，匙叉在你吃東西的時候也會很有用！GPS，簡單的急救組…你不可能會準備過頭。

一問三答 MP3 086

17 Question

What is your best camping experience?
你最棒的露營經驗是什麼呢？

To be honest, I haven't really camped that many times yet, but I'll say that the time when I was at Uluru was pretty good. I went with the luxurious package where we had Champaign and buffet right in front of Uluru. I cannot imagine anyone who doesn't do this when they finish the day hike there. Oh and did I mention the camel ride before that?

老實說，我還沒有露營很多次，但我可以說我在烏魯魯的時候還蠻不錯的。我選了奢華旅行行程。我們在烏魯魯前喝香檳和吃 buffet。我無法想像任何人在健行完之後不選擇這個行程。喔我有提到還有騎駱駝嗎？

I had a blast when I was at Jasper National Park last year. There are countless beautiful lakes where you can go kayaking, fishing, white water rafting, etc. You name it. I met some really cool world travelers at the campsite that evening. We spent our evening playing music and share stories under the stars.

我去年在賈斯柏國家公園裡玩得很開心。那裡有數不清的湖泊，在那裡你可以划塑膠皮艇、釣魚，和泛舟等等。你說的出來的都有。我那天晚上在營地也遇到很多很酷的正在環遊世界的人。我們那天晚上就在星空下玩音樂和分享彼此的故事中度過。

Becca
貝卡

I scored big when I was in Yosemite National Park. Camping is relatively affordable for accommodation already. However, the fee to camp at Yosemite ranged from 6 to 26 dollars per night. I managed to secure a week for only 6 dollars per night. That was an unforgettable experience camping at such a beautiful place with so little expense. I was very pleased.

我在優美聖地國家公園裡拿到超好的優惠。露營本來就在住宿裡算比較負擔得起的了。但是在優美聖地裡露營的費用從六塊美金到二十六塊美金一個晚上不等。我竟然預訂到了一個禮拜每天晚上六元美金的而已。用那麼少的花費在那麼美的地方露營真是一個難忘的經驗。我超滿意的。

一問三答 MP3 087

18 Question

What is the best hike you have ever done? How was it?

你健行過最好的步道是哪裡？那個步道怎麼樣呢？

Michelle 蜜雪兒

The best hike I have ever had or done is the Inca Hike in Peru. Don't get me wrong, I enjoy hiking, but it just needs to be fine-tuned. I joined this luxurious package where you get to get gourmet meals with champaign every night, and enjoy the only hot showers on the trail. What's better? I got massages every night when I was on the trail. I thought that was an excellent remedy for my aching muscles. That was a pretty good hiking experience.

我去過或唯一健行過最棒的步道是秘魯的印加古道。別誤會我喔，健行這個活動只要微調一下，我其實是喜歡健行的。我有參加這個豪華的行程，每天都可以吃美食加上香檳，然後享用步道上唯一的熱水澡。更棒的是什麼？我每天晚上都有按摩。那真是對我健行後痠痛的肌肉很好的治療。那個健行的經驗是還不錯啦。

Matt
麥特

The best hike I've ever done is the trek to Everest Base Camp in Nepal. The people are incredible. The scenery can't be beat, and you get to take a look at Mt. Everest or Chomolungma, which means the "Goddess Mother of the World." It's spectacular just to see the highest point on planet Earth. In May, the rhododendrons are in bloom with orchids growing in them. There are guesthouses on the way up. You can get a beer. Who knows, I might wander up there again.

我去過最棒的是尼泊爾的聖母峰基地營健行。那裡的人都好得不可思議，無敵的風景，而且你還可以看到聖母峰，或是 Chomolungma（聖母峰藏文），也就是世界之母的意思。可以從世界最高點看下去真的是很壯觀。在五月的時候，杜鵑花會和蘭花一起盛開。在上去的路上也會遇到民宿，而你也可以在那買瓶啤酒。誰知道，我可能會在遊蕩上去一次。

Becca
貝卡

No doubt the hike that circles Mont Blanc—the rooftop of Western Europe—is one of the best hiking experiences I have ever had. You travel through three different countries (France, Italy, Switzerland). But it's the civilization in between that really makes the trail special. Stop at villages or huts along the way to gorge yourself with fondue, wine, slices of local cheeses, and homemade bread—then keep walking to work it all off. It's all about motivations, isn't it?

毫無疑問那個環繞勃朗峰的步道，西歐的屋脊，是我最棒的健行經驗之一。你會經過三個不一樣的國家（法國、義大利和瑞士）。但是讓這個步道很特別的地方是在步道中的文明。你可以停留在小鎮或是路上的小茅屋去吃起司鍋、喝美酒、或是一片當地的起司，和手工作的麵包，然後再繼續往前走去把這些熱量都消耗掉。健行就是要有動力，不是嗎？

一問三答 MP3 088

19 Question

Why do you think people like fishing as a hobby?

你覺得為什麼會有人把釣魚當作一種興趣？

Michelle
蜜雪兒

I know, right? Why do people like fishing as a hobby!...Oh wait, are you asking me? Hmm...I don't know. It's still a mystery to me. You beat me on this one. My best bet is that people are just running out of things to do. I don't have a clue on this one.

對啊，我知道。怎麼會有人把釣魚當作一種興趣！…喔你是在問我嗎？嗯…我不知道耶。對我來說還是一個謎。這題你真的考倒我了。我最好的猜測就是他們沒其他的事可以做了。我真的一點都不曉得。

Why would anyone not like fishing as a hobby is the real question to ask here. It's fun, and it can be both exciting and relaxing. You can possibly catch your own meals, and it's guaranteed fresh catch. Besides, it's extremely addicting. Once you try and you like it, it stays with you for a while.

怎麼會有人不把釣魚當作一種興趣才是真正要問的問題。它又好玩，既刺激又休閒。你有可能會抓到自己的食物而且還保證新鮮。除此之外，它真的是超級令人上癮。只要你試過一次，而且你也喜歡的話，你就會喜歡好長一陣子。

I can see why people like fishing as a hobby. It's pretty mellow and you really don't need much to entertain yourself. Just a fishing pole with baits, a cooler and yourself. We're lucky that we can enjoy fishing differently than a lot of fishermen did back then. It must have been just catching and catching some more. I can see where the excitement comes when you catch one, too.

我可以懂為什麼大家喜歡把釣魚當作一種興趣。很放鬆而且你真的不需要太多東西來娛樂自己。只要有釣魚竿和餌，一個小冰箱和你自己。我們跟很多以前的漁夫比起來真的很幸運因為我們可以享受釣魚。我想以前大概就是釣魚，在釣多一點魚。我也可以理解為什麼釣魚很刺激。

一問三答 MP3 089

20 Question

Have you been to any sports game? How was it?

你有去看過任何運動的比賽嗎？好玩嗎？

Michelle 蜜雪兒

I was invited to the 2015 FIFA Women's World Cup in Canada because a friend I grew up with was playing for USA. I got the VIP seats to watch the game and joined them for the after party to celebrate the victory. It was quite an experience to witness my friend add World Cup Champion to her already amazing career.

我有一個從小長大的朋友他代表美國隊參賽，所以我受邀去加拿大看 2015 年的女子世界盃足球賽。我有 VIP 座位，而且後來還加入她們慶祝勝利的派對。親眼看到我朋友把世足冠軍列入她本來就很好的職業生涯真的是很棒的經驗。

Matt 麥特

I went on a road trip in California. It was during the time of the NBA playoffs, we couldn't pass the game in Los Angeles when the Lakers are playing against the Miami Heat. It was quite an exciting game to watch. You can't beat live NBA playoffs. It was totally worth the drive.

我到加州公路旅行，那個時候正好是 NBA 季後賽的時候，所以我們不想錯過在加州的湖人隊跟邁阿密熱火隊的賽事。那場比賽真的很刺激，而且你真的無法超越現場的 NBA 季後賽。完全值得我們開那麼遠的車去看。

I watched a college volleyball game in Italy when I was doing the exchange student program. I didn't know what to expect, but they were actually really skilled. Apparently, it has become a very popular sport in Italy. It was really fun watching the game for sure.

我在義大利當交換學生的時候去看了一場大學排球賽。我不知道該預期什麼，但是他們真的很厲害耶。很顯然的在義大利，排球已經漸漸成為一個蠻受歡迎的運動。至少是很好看的比賽。

一問三答 MP3 090

21 Question

Which was one special sport you tried on your trip? Did you like it?

你有在旅行的時候嘗試過什麼特別的運動嗎？你喜歡嗎？

Michelle
蜜雪兒

I tried Aerial Yoga in New York City when I was on a business trip last time. It definitely turned my world upside down. It's basically the combination of Yoga and Pilates with the use of a hammock. I felt really good after the workout.

我上次去紐約市出差的時候有試過空中瑜珈。那真的是把我的世界弄得翻天覆地的。那其實就是用吊床來練習瑜珈和皮拉提斯的綜合版。我在運動後真的覺得很棒。

Matt
麥特

I tried wake surfing in Moscow. It's really cool because you are basically surfing the wake created by the boat in front of you. Who knows that you can surf in a lake as well? I mean it's nothing crazy, but it's awesome to get on your board and have some fun.

我在莫斯科有嘗試尾流衝浪。那很酷因為你就是在衝你前面的船幫你製造出來的浪。誰知道你也可以在湖上衝浪？我是說，那沒有衝很瘋狂的浪還是什麼的，可是可以拿你的板子出來就玩得很開心真的很棒。

Becca
貝卡

I tried Capoeira when I was in Brazil. It was really spontaneous because I was walking down the street from my hostel when I ran into a group of people circled together doing this thing called Capoeira. It was somewhere between martial art and awkward dancing. One of them actually asked me to try it with them. I did! He might have regretted inviting me to do it because I had no idea what I was doing, but I'm glad I tried!

我去巴西的時候有試過卡波耶拉。那真的很隨性因為我只是從我的青年旅社走出來，然後就遇到一群人圍成一個圈圈在做這個叫做卡波耶拉的運動。那其實有點是在武術和很拙劣的舞蹈中間。他們其中一個人叫我加入他們一起嘗試看看，然後我就試試看了。他可能有後悔邀請我一起因為我真的不知道我在幹嘛，但是我還是很高興我試了一下。

一問三答 MP3 091

22 Question

What sport do you want to learn? Why?

你有特別想要學什麼運動嗎？為什麼？

I've always wanted to try horseback riding. What's not to love about horses? I loved riding the ponies ever since I was a child, but there's a fine line between reality and fantasy. There were several times when I finally decided to do it, I chickened out the second I went on the horseback. Oh well...

我一直以來都很想學騎馬。馬有什麼值得你討厭的？我從小就很喜歡騎小馬，但是現實跟幻想之間就是有點不同。有好幾次我終於決定要去學，可是一騎上馬背我就退縮了。就是這樣囉...。

I want to get into rock climbing. I think it's such a great exercise and it'll be a good skill to have when I'm traveling. You never know. I also heard that helps you to become stronger as a person as well. There are a lot of fear factors when you are dangling from high above, and you just have to take the leap of faith to get to the next step!

我想要學攀岩。我想那會是一個很好的經驗，而且在旅行的時候那也會是一個很好的技能。一切都很難說。而且我聽說攀岩也可以幫助你成為一個更堅強的人。當你懸逛在高處的時候，有很多令你害怕的事情，可是你就是要有信心地跳躍過去下一步。

Becca
貝卡

I think Zumba will be a good sport to learn! I tried it once in Panama, and I really had so much fun even if I had no idea what I was doing. It's pretty much a dancing sport. I think it'll be something I'll stay interested in for a while. And did I mention the music rocks?

我覺得尊巴會是一個很好的運動！我有在巴拿馬試過一次。就算我當時一點都不知道我在幹嘛，可是我還是玩得好開心。那其實就是一個跳舞的運動。我想那是一個我會喜歡蠻久的運動。而且我有說尊巴的音樂超棒的嗎？

一問三答 MP3 092

23 Question What is your favorite water sport? Why?
你最喜歡的水上活動是什麼？為什麼呢？

Michelle 蜜雪兒

I don't like water sports...If I really have to pick one, I would probably go with snorkeling. It's pretty cool to peek in what's under the ocean without getting too involved. There are a lot of hotels that have snorkeling packages you can join or some hotels even have a pool you can swim with fish. If you want, of course.

我不喜歡水上活動...不過如果真的硬要選，我應該會選浮潛吧！可以看看海裡面有什麼是還蠻酷的，而且也沒有跟他們太近。很多飯店都會有浮潛的行程可以加入。有的飯店還會有游泳池是你可以在裡面浮潛，跟魚一起游泳的。當然是你想要的話啦！

Matt 麥特

My favorite water sport is definitely surfing. Nothing else can make you feel so free. And I'm more focused on the moment when I'm surfing.

You have to observe your surroundings constantly and live in that moment because once you daydream, the wave is gone already. I learned a lot about life from surfing. Like how you should always be humble facing the ocean and I like to think of the ocean as life in this case.

　　我最喜歡的水上活動一定是衝浪。沒有任何事可以讓你覺得那麼自由自在。而且我在衝浪的時候會更專注在當下。你要一直觀察你周遭的環境，然後活在當下因為你只要一發呆，浪就過了。我從衝浪學了很多關於人生的道理。例如你面對海洋的時候一定要保持謙卑，而在這個例子裡，我也喜歡把海洋想成人生。

　　My favorite water sport is diving. I love going diving when I'm troubled with life. Every single noise just instantly goes away once I'm in the water. I can only hear my breath and the bubbles I created from the oxygen tank. It's a really relaxing and peaceful feeling down there.

　　我最喜歡的水上活動是潛水。每次我人生遇到難題的時候我就會去潛水。一下水，每個雜音都立刻消失。我只聽得到我呼吸的聲音和從氧氣筒呼吸時製造的泡泡聲。在水裡真的是很放鬆又很平靜的感覺。

一問三答 MP3 093

24 Question

Do you know a secret spot for any water sport?

你知道任何水上活動的秘密地點嗎？

Michelle
蜜雪兒

I don't think it's a secret, but the Great Barrier Reef in Australia is always something people talk about when it comes to snorkeling or other water sports. Remember the campaign for the best job in the world back in 2009? The job was to take care of the Great Barrier Reef. I don't want to admit it, but I applied for the job as well...

我覺得這個應該不是秘密了，不過每次提到浮潛還是其他水上活動，大家就會提到澳洲的大堡礁。還記得 2009 年那個全世界最棒的工作的宣傳嗎？那個工作就是可以照顧大堡礁。我不想承認，可是我那時候也有應徵那個工作啦…

Matt
麥特

Have you heard about "Cloud 9"? It's a really good surf spot in the Philippines. They have some world-class waves there. It's not as crowded as many famous surf spots, and there are a lot of bed and breakfast there where you can stay for a cheap price with healthy meals there. I really enjoy my stay there every time I go.

你有聽過「Cloud 9」嗎？那是在菲律賓很有名的衝浪點。那裡不像很多其他有名的浪點一樣擁擠，在那裡你付很少錢就可以住在那裡的民宿，而且那裡還有提供健康的餐點。我每次去都玩得很開心。

There are a lot of turtle cleaning stations in the Hawaiian Islands. The turtle cleaning stations are just huge flat rocks where turtles just come and sit on the rock and the little fish will come and clean their shells. It's really cool to watch them come in and get cleaned.

在夏威夷群島裡有很多的烏龜清洗站。烏龜清洗站其實就是一塊平坦的大石頭，烏龜們會來坐在那石頭上，然後很多小魚就會來清洗龜殼上的髒東西。看到烏龜們游來清洗他們的殼的時候真的很神奇。

一問三答 MP3 094

25 Question What is the scariest experience you had with water sports?

你有過最恐怖的水上活動的經驗是什麼？

Scariest one was when I stood up paddling with some of my girlfriends in Panama right in front of our resort. We were just enjoying ourselves out there when one of my friends screamed out “sharks!!” and pointed to the fins on the surface of the water. We all screamed together and tried to paddle away from it. We ended up paddling to a school of dolphins. It was truly a blessing in disguise.

最恐怖的就是我跟一些女生朋友在巴拿馬渡假飯店前站立式划槳的時候。當我們正玩得開心時，其中一個朋友突然尖叫：鯊魚！然後指著水裡的鰭。我們一起尖叫，然後儘快划離開那些鰭。結果我們到最後划著遇到一群海豚。那真的是因禍得福。

One time my buddy and I went kayaking, and the wind started to take us away from the shore very fast. We were drifting very fast from the shore. It was till the point when it was getting dark that we thought there was no way for us to paddle back. We called the Coast Guard for rescue. They sent in a helicopter to locate us and then a boat came and towed us back. It was a very close call.

有一次我跟我的好朋友在划皮艇，結果風突然很快的把我們吹離岸邊。我們很快的漂離了很遠。直到天黑了我們才認知到我們已經划不回岸邊了。我們得打給海岸警備隊求救。他們叫了一架直升機來幫我們定位，然後一艘船再來把我們拖回去。當下真的很危急。

When I was in Costa Rica. I signed up for a surfing lesson by the beach there. I had a lot of butterflies in my stomach before I went. Everything went very well, and it was such a fun experience until a set of big waves came in and washed me down in the water. The current was so strong that I was just tumbling in the waves. It felt like I was in a washing machine. Luckily, my surf instructor came and got me out of the water very fast.

我在哥斯大黎加的時候有在那裡的海邊報名衝浪課程。我在去之前很緊張，但是去了之後一切都很順利，而且也很好玩，直到突然有一陣陣的大浪來了，然後把我衝到水裡。水裡的急流很強，所以我就一直在浪裡翻滾。我那時候覺得我好像在洗衣機裡面一樣。好險我的衝浪教練及時把我從水裡很快的拉出來。

一問三答 MP3 095

26 Question

What is your favorite type of music?

你最喜歡的是哪一類的音樂呢？

My favorite type of music is Jazz. It's the perfect music in the morning, in the afternoon and in the evening. I just can't get enough of it. There are so many emotions in Jazz and I always feel like when people are talking about music being contagious, I think they are referring to Jazz.

我最喜歡的音樂就是爵士樂。早上、下午和晚上聽都很棒。我就是聽不膩爵士啦。爵士樂裡有很多的情緒。當大家在說音樂很有感染力的時候，我都想說他們一定是在說爵士樂。

I'm gonna go with Reggae. I've been traveling in a lot of islands, and they start to grow on me one day, and before I know it, I'm humming the reggae tunes all day. It's a very relaxing, beach music really. I'm not too big of a dancer, either, but I can do the swing with

Reggae music.

我應該是會選雷鬼樂。我已經在很多的島嶼旅行過了。突然有一天我漸漸開始喜歡雷鬼樂，然後在我反應過來之前，我已經整天都在哼雷鬼的調子了。那是一種很令人放鬆，海邊的那種音樂。我也不是很會跳舞，但是我可以跟著雷鬼樂搖擺。

I think all my favorite songs belong to Indie Rock, so I assume that's my favorite type of music. You know how sometimes when you turn on the radio, and you just connect with the tunes, I think Indie Rock is my tune.

我覺得好像我很喜歡的歌都是獨立搖滾，所以我想那應該是我最喜歡的音樂種類吧！你知道有的時候你打開電台音樂，然後你就會蠻喜歡某一台的音樂，我想我喜歡的那台就是獨立搖滾。

一問三答 MP3 096

27 Question

Where have you heard the best live music?

你在哪裡聽過最棒的現場的音樂？

The best one was at the Preservation Hall in New Orleans. It's like the holy ground for all jazz fans. I had my doubts before it started because it was in a tiny and old building with no seats or air-conditioning, but when they started to perform, I had goose bumps, and I was listening in tears. Let's just put it that way.

我聽過最棒的是在紐奧良的典藏廳。那裡就像是爵士樂迷們的聖地一樣。我在表演開始之前有我的疑慮因為那棟建築又小又舊而且又沒有座位和冷氣。可是當他們開始演奏的時候，我全身起雞皮疙瘩，還含淚聽整個表演。這樣說你就懂了吧。

I was backpacking in New Zealand when my CouchSurfing host took me to this family fair. It was really fun with a lot of rides and food stands, but what caught my attention was this reggae band that was playing on stage. They are called Ketchafire and that was the best live music I've ever heard. It was just amazing really.

我在紐西蘭當背包客的時候，我沙發衝浪的主人帶我去一個家庭園遊會。那裡真的很好玩，而且也有很多遊樂設施和小吃攤，但是真正讓我注意到的是正在台上表演的雷鬼樂團。他們的名字是 Ketchafire 而那也是我聽過最棒的現場的音樂。真的很棒！

I was walking at the underground of a park in Spain and that was when I came across this amazing street artist. He's a guitarist, and really all he did was just playing guitar, but the sound was very crisp with the echoes from the underground, it became very powerful music. There were people stopping here and there, but I stayed the whole time. I couldn't leave such a great performance. Of course, I gave him some money afterwards and bought the CD. The CD isn't quite the same as what I heard that day, but it's still great.

我在西班牙一個公園的地下道走路時，突然遇到這個超厲害的街頭藝人。他是一個吉他手，然後他真的也只是就是在彈吉他而已，但是吉他的聲音很清脆，而且因為在地下道有回音就讓整個音樂十分的強烈。我那時候停下來就走不開這個表演了。當然，我後來有給他一些錢還有買了他的 CD。CD 跟現場聽的時候不一樣，可是還是很棒。

一問三答 MP3 097

28 Question

What's the most unique experience you have related to music?

你有關於音樂最獨特的經驗嗎？

Michelle 蜜雪兒

I was visiting some friends in Bogota, Colombia, and one night we went to this tiny bar where there was a singer singing some Latin love songs in the bar. Everything looked very normal until the singer walked to my friends, and asked them in Spanish what kind of music I like, I told him Reggaeton, which is like the Spanish version of Hip-Pop I really like back then. He walked back and talked to other musicians, and then he started to sing my favorite Reggaeton song. The whole bar started to dance and he came singing to me and danced with me!

我在哥倫比亞・波哥大拜訪朋友的時候，有一天晚上我們去一個很小的酒吧，台上有一個歌手正在唱著拉丁的情歌。一切看起來都很正常，直到那個歌手走向我的朋友並用西班牙文問他們我喜歡哪一種音樂，我跟他說雷鬼動，也就是我以前很喜歡的很像是西文版的嘻哈音樂。他走回去樂團跟其他樂手說話，然後他就開始唱了我最喜歡的雷鬼動的歌。整個酒吧都在跳舞，他還來對我唱歌，並跟我一起跳舞。

I was visiting the Finger Lake area and my friends told me about the Flotilla they were doing on one of the finger lake for 4th of July. Everyone took out their boats and tied them together. They had some performers played live music together and just enjoyed a good day on the lake. That was pretty cool for me to see.

當我獨立紀念日在手指湖的時候，我的朋友跟我說他們在獨立紀念日那天有 Flotilla（小型艦隊）這個活動。大家都把他們的船開出來，然後綁在一起。他們有請一些表演者來表演一些現場音樂，然後就享受那美好的一天。我那時候覺得真的超酷的。

I went to Taiwan and found out this local's favorite hangout, KTV, which stands for Kareoke Television. You can reserve a room with a big TV screen, and order songs from the computer system and sing them with your friends. It's really fun because you are not singing in front of a bunch of people you don't know. You can order food and drinks, too. I thought that was so cool.

我去台灣的時候發現當地人最喜歡去的地方是 KTV。你可以訂一個包廂，裡面有很大的電視銀幕。你可以從電腦系統裡面點歌，然後跟你的朋友一起唱歌。真的很好玩因為你不是在一群你不認識的人裡面唱歌。你還可以點吃的跟喝的。我覺得很酷。

一問三答 MP3 098

29 Question

Do you enjoy festivals? Why? Why not?

你喜歡節慶嘛？為什麼喜歡或是為什麼不喜歡？

Michelle
蜜雪兒

I'm not a festival person per say. I don't think I like it that much mainly because of the crowds a festival brings. If people can just keep a safe distance and mind their own business, then I might be fine with it, but that's not usually the case. Too many people just make everything worse. The traffic is bad, the bathrooms are dirty, and people get injured all the time in a festival. I'd rather stay at home and watch TV I think.

我本身沒有很喜歡節慶啦。我覺得我不喜歡的原因主要是因為節慶都會有很多人。如果大家可以保持安全距離，或是只管他們自己的閒事的話，那我就還可以參加，可是通常都不是那樣。人太多就會把一切搞砸。交通會很塞，廁所會變得很髒，很多人參加慶典也都會受傷。我覺得我寧願在家看電視。

I'm all about it. I love everything about a festival. The smell, the people, the music, the food, and the dance...I can go on and on about this all day. I always feel so alive when I'm in one of those events. It makes me feel like I'm a little kid again, and it's okay, too. Love it.

我最喜歡節慶了！我喜歡關於節慶的每一件事。節慶的味道、人群、音樂、食物和跳舞...我可以一直說下去。我每次參加這類的活動時就會覺得我是活著的。它讓我覺得我好像又變成一個小孩子，而且那樣也沒關係。超棒的。

You know, I've been there and done that. I think it's cool to check it out, but I'm just over the party scenes. I'm at that age where most of my friends hang out at the coffee shops instead of clubs. I guess I'm just having the quarter life crisis. Haha... I'm usually ready to go to bed when it hits 10:30. I guess if the festivals are in the daytime, I want to check it out, but if not, I won't cry my heart out.

你知道，我已經做過那些事了。我是覺得去看看是不錯，可是我已經不party了。我已經到了那個大多數的朋友都會在咖啡店而不是在夜店裡的年紀了。我想我現在應該是有四分之一年危機（25 歲）。哈哈...而且我通常十點半就會去睡了。如果那些節慶是在白天的話，我會去看看，不然沒去的話我也不會傷心的要命啦。

一問三答 MP3 099

30 Question

What is the most impressive festival you have ever been to?

你去過最令你印象深刻的節慶是什麼？

Michelle 蜜雪兒

I went to the Carnival of Venice, and it was such a gorgeous festival. Everyone dressed up nicely and wore these amazing masks. I had to buy so many of those masks before I left Venice. There were fireworks by the canal, too. Very impressive and when can you dress up like that with so many people anyways?

我去了威尼斯的嘉年華會。那個節慶真是超美的。大家都精心打扮然後還帶了很棒的面具。我在離開威尼斯之前不得不買了很多面具。在運河旁也有放煙火。超令人印象深刻的，而且你還可以去哪裡精心打扮成那樣？

Matt 麥特

The most impressive festival I've ever been to is the Oktoberfest in

Munich. It was a pretty big event, and I always thought Oktoberfest is all about beer drinking, but to my surprise, there are water slides, fun rides, food stands and then there are the big tents for beers and pretzels. It was really fun to see how people dressed in traditional German outfits. I had such a great time there!

我去過最令我印象深刻的節慶是在慕尼黑的啤酒節。那是一個蠻大的節慶，而且我一直以為啤酒節就只是喝啤酒而已，可是令我很意外的是那裡有很多滑水道、遊樂設施、食物的攤販。然後你才會看到他們有設立一些大帳篷，裡面你才可以喝啤酒和吃扭結餅。看大家穿著德國傳統的服飾真的很好玩，我玩得超開心的。

I went and celebrated the festival of lights, or Diwali, with my friends in India. It was actually the Hindu New Year, so in a way, it was their New Year celebration. It was really impressive because besides the big fireworks to start with, there were candles everywhere. Every household decorated their houses, too. It was just a very stunning festival to participate in.

我在印度跟我的朋友一起慶祝了排燈節，而那時候正是印度教的新年，所以其實也就是他們新年的慶典。那個節慶很令人印象深刻因為除了一開始的時候有盛大的煙火，也有隨處可見的蠟燭。每家每戶也都會佈置他們的房子。那真是一個很美的節日。

一問三答 MP3 100

31 Question What is the strangest festival you have ever heard of?
你聽過最奇怪的節慶是什麼呢？

The Songkran Festival in Thailand is pretty bizarre for me. They dump water on each other during the New Year celebration. It's said that they do this to wash away the bad luck or bad spirits away...I think they might have taken that a little too literally.

我覺得泰國的潑水節真的對我來說很奇怪。他們會在新年的時候互相潑彼此水。據說他們是想要潑掉厄運或是邪靈…可是我覺得他們好像真的想得太簡單和直接了。

I heard about this festival in Thailand. It's called the monkey festival. What the locals do is that they lay out the fruits to attract a lot of monkeys. The strange part is that they only do this to boost the tourism. Weird, isn't it?

我聽說在泰國有一個節叫做猴子節。當地人會把很多水果擺出來吸引猴子。我覺得奇怪的點是他這個節日完全只是因為要吸引遊客而產生的。很奇怪吧？

The strangest festival I've heard of is the Day of the Dead that's celebrated in Mexico. At the beginning, it's strange for me that people "celebrate" the fact that their family is dead, but then I thought that is such a good idea. On this day, the families gather together, have fun and share stories about their family that had passed away. A strange but good idea!

我聽過最奇怪的節是墨西哥的亡靈節。一開始的時候我覺得很奇怪，為什麼他們要「慶祝」亡靈，可是我後來覺得這真的是蠻好的點子。在這天，家人會聚在一起玩樂，和互相分享死去的家人故事。很奇怪，但是是個好主意。

一問三答 MP3 101

32 Question

What type of performances or shows do you enjoy? Why?

你喜歡哪一種表演或是秀呢？為什麼？

I love going to the magic and acrobatic shows. It just never gets old for me. I love it ever since I was little and I still do. Without those performances and performers, this world is going to be so dull. There is always a joyful atmosphere and full of surprises in those performances, and I guess that's why I love it.

我最喜歡魔術或是雜耍的表演。我都看不膩那些。而且我從小就很喜歡看那些表演。我覺得如果沒有那些表演和表演者的話，這個世界會變得很乏味。在那些表演中總是有很歡樂的氣氛而且也充滿了驚喜。我想那就是為什麼我喜歡它們的原因了。

I think the best kind of performances usually comes from the street. There are so many street artists on the road, and many of them are truly talented. They rely the least on other equipment, too. Also, it's the easiest way to engage in a performance, and also to leave one if you don't enjoy them. I think they are the hidden gems of performances.

我覺得最好的表演通常都來自街上。在街上有那麼多的街頭藝人，而且其實他們很多人都真的很有才華！他們也是仰賴任何其他的配備最少的人。另外，我覺得看街頭表演是最容易加入的一種表演，還有如果你不喜歡的話，也是最容易離開的。我個人認為那是表演裡的隱藏珍寶！

I really enjoy musicals. It's live concert mixed with drama and great choreography, too. Musicals are great treats to all our senses. Those performers can pretty much do everything, and they have not failed me so far. A lot is going on when you are watching a musical. I love it. It is like a combination of birthday party and Christmas.

我最喜歡歌舞劇。因為它就是現場演唱會，加上戲劇和超棒的編舞啊！音樂劇對我們的感官是極大的享受。那些表演者真的什麼都可以表演的出來，而且他們目前為止也沒有讓我失望。在看舞台劇的時候會覺得那個表演很豐富。我超愛的，就像是生日舞會加上聖誕節一樣。

一問三答 MP3 102

33 Question

Have you been to any one-of -a kind performance? Where was it?

你有去過哪一個獨一無二的表演呢？那是在哪裡？

When I went to my sister's graduation in Hawaii, we went to the Polynesian Cultural Center, and we watched the night performance that consisted of all different tribes of people in Hawaii. There were Hawaiian, Tahitian, Samoan, Tong Ga...etc. And the show was fantastic, and I don't think I would be able to see it anywhere else.

我去夏威夷參加我妹妹的畢業典禮時，我們去了波里尼西亞文化中心看了一個在晚上的表演。它綜合了夏威夷各族人。有夏威夷人、大溪地人、薩摩爾和東加...等等。那個秀真的棒透了，而我也覺得那是在別的地方看不到的表演。

I was once traveling in Manhattan and of course I had to check out Time Square. Just when I was taking some pictures there, there was one guy started singing “just the way you are” by Bruno Mars, and then more people joined him and they all started dancing. I quickly realized they are the flash mobs! I recorded the whole thing right away. After they finished, everyone cheered and they went different directions. I thought I was so lucky.

我在曼哈頓旅行的時候，當然得去時代廣場看看。就在我在那裡照相的時候，突然有個男的開始唱火星人布魯諾的「Just the way you are」，然後越來越多人加入他唱歌和跳舞。我馬上就想到他們就是快閃族！我立刻全程錄影。他們結束後，大家就歡呼，然後他們就往不同的方向離開了。我那時候覺得我真的超幸運的！

I went to an impromptu comedy when I was in Amsterdam. Usually, I go to standup comedy shows, but rarely do I go to the impromptu comedies. What it was was that they improvised the show as they go. Usually they perform the interaction between them and the audience. There was no script. I thought that was really impressive and literally one-of-a-kind!

我去了阿姆斯特丹的即興喜劇表演。我通常都只是去喜劇表演，超少去即興喜劇表演。那其實就是他們全程都是即興表演。通常是從跟觀眾或是他們自己本身的互動中延伸出來的。完全沒有劇本。我覺得那是很令人印象深刻還有真的是獨一無二的表演。

一問三答 MP3 103

34 Question What was your worst experience in an amusement park?

你在遊樂園裡最糟的經驗是什麼？

I would dedicate my worst experience to the Haunted House at L.A. Universal Studio. Their problem was that they took everything way too seriously. It was a walking tour through the whole haunted house. Everything in the haunted house was as if they came out directly from the crime scene. I had nightmares and was scarred to go to any haunted house after that one.

我要把我在遊樂園最糟的經驗頒給在洛杉磯環球影城的鬼屋。他們的問題就是他們太認真了啦。那是一個要走路穿過鬼屋的行程。每一個在那個鬼屋裡面的東西都好像是直接從犯罪現場搬來的。我再去玩那個鬼屋之後就做惡夢，而且還從此對鬼屋有陰影。

I've never really had a bad experience in the amusement park although there was one time when we were stuck on the Ferris wheel for an hour. I didn't mind it, but it gets scary because we didn't know when we could get back to the ground. It was pretty windy up there, too. Then, I started to have flashbacks about those horrifying scenes from the scary movies.

我在遊樂園裡沒有什麼不好的經驗，不過有一次我在摩天輪上面卡了一個小時。我一開始是不介意，但是後來越來越可怕因為我們不知道什麼時候才可以回到陸地上。而且在上面的時候風也很大。然後我腦海就開始有一些恐怖片裡面的恐怖情節畫面。

My worst experience was actually kind of funny. I got motion sickness when I was on a roller coaster ride. My best friend at the time was nice enough to sit me down at the chair nearby and listened to how dizzy I felt the whole time. To my surprise, she was the one that puked at the end. I felt very bad for her, but wasn't I the sick one?

我最不好的經驗其實還蠻好笑的。我坐完雲霄飛車的時候開始有點暈。我那時候最好的朋友人很好的帶我去坐在附近的椅子上，而且還全程一直聽我說我有多暈。嚇到我的是，後來是她在吐。我覺得蠻對不起她的，可是我才是不舒服的人，不是嗎？

一問三答 MP3 104

35 Question

Have you ever been on any cruise? How was it?

你有搭過遊輪嗎？結果怎麼樣？

Michelle 蜜雪兒

I went on a cruise for a friend's wedding. Their wedding was a destination wedding, and the ship took everyone to Hawaii and that's where my friends had the ceremony. It was a perfect way to get everyone together and celebrate their wedding together. It was the best wedding party I've ever been to. However, I have to say that perhaps there is a reason why normally the wedding is only 1 day! I can't handle partying for a week! It's just too much.

我有在遊輪上面慶祝我朋友的婚禮。他們的婚禮是一個度假婚禮。遊輪帶大家去夏威夷參加他們的結婚典禮。那是一個很完美的辦法把大家聚在一起，並且一起慶祝他們的婚禮。那是我去過最棒的婚禮，可是我必須說或許一般的婚禮都只有一天是有原因的！我實在是沒有辦法狂歡一個禮拜！太累了啦！

Matt 麥特

I have a buddy who works for a cruise ship, so he pulled some string and got me a ticket to a short cruise to Alaska. It was so nice and the cruise was beautiful. When we got to Alaska, we even went sports fishing. I had a blast and even if half of the time I was seasick, it was still a great experience.

我有一個好朋友在遊輪上工作，於是他就動用了一些關係幫我拿到一張短程去阿拉斯加的遊輪。整個旅程很好而且那段路也十分的美麗。當我們到阿拉斯加的時候，我們還去釣魚。即使一半的行程我都在暈船，我還是玩得很開心。那是一個很棒的經驗。

I went on a sunset cruise at the Darling Harbour at Sydney. It was really romantic and the sunset was beautiful. I did notice there were a lot of couples, and so it was a little bit weird. Other than that, the food is great, and they also have drinks on board, too. It was really nice to tour around Darling Harbour and frankly I think that's the best way!

我在雪梨的時候去了達令港坐日落遊輪。我覺得很浪漫而且日落也好美。我的確是有注意到很多的情侶，所以那有點奇怪。除了那樣之外，食物很好吃，而且他們船上也有喝的。我覺得用遊輪觀光達令港是一個蠻棒的方式，老實說，我覺得是最棒的方式。

一問三答 MP3 105

36 Question

Which traditional costumes would you like to try on? Why?

世界上所有的傳統服飾裡你有想要試穿哪一個嗎？為什麼？

Michelle
蜜雪兒

I would love to try on the Flamenco dresses from Andalucía, Spain. They are just so bright-colored and passionate. I saw a few Flamenco dancers performing at the mall, and I thought their costumes are so beautiful. Hey, you know what? I'm gonna be a Flamenco Dancer this Halloween! Thanks for the inspiration! I think I can rock the outfit!

我會想要試試看西班牙安達魯西亞的佛朗明哥裙。它們是那麼的鮮豔和熱情。我有在購物中心看過一些佛朗明歌舞者表演，然後我就在想他們的服裝都好美喔！喔你知道怎樣嗎？我今年的萬聖節要打扮成佛朗明哥舞者！謝謝你給我的靈感！我覺得我一定可以穿得很好看的！

Matt
麥特

I want to try on the Kilts from Scotland! Honestly I've never tried on a skirt in my life. When I first heard about the costume, my friends and I thought that was so ridiculous. Why do men in Scotland wear skirts? However, just because of that, I really want to try it so that I can say I've tried on a Kilt before. And I'm curious about how it feels to be in a skirt. Must be pretty breezy...

我想要試試看蘇格蘭的蘇格蘭裙！老實說，我從來都沒穿過裙子。一開始聽到蘇格蘭裙的時候，我跟我的朋友就想說那真是太荒謬了。蘇格蘭的男人怎麼會穿裙子啊？但是也是因為那樣，我真的很想要試試看，然後我就可以說我有穿過蘇格蘭裙了。而且其實我很好奇穿裙子是什麼感覺。一定很涼...。

I was in Indian, but I didn't get to try on the Sari there. I did go to the markets, and there are a lot of Sari shops there, and may I just say that the Saris are gorgeous! You can even mix and match your own fabric! I was in a hurry, so I didn't get to try on anything, but if I could go back in time, I would totally try it on!

我有去印度，可是我沒有試穿到紗麗。我有去那裡的市集，那裡有很多賣紗麗的店，而且我可以說紗麗真的是很美嘛！你還可以混搭不同的布料來做你的紗麗！我那時候很趕，所以我不能試穿任何一個，可是如果我可以回到當時的話，我一定會試穿的！

一問三答 MP3 106

37 Question

Have you ever felt like you need to change the way you dress when you travel?

你有沒有曾經在旅行的時候覺得你應該要改變你打扮的方式？

Michelle 蜜雪兒

When I was in Milan last year, the first day I was there, I felt like I needed a makeover ASAP! That was the only day I dressed down, and that was the worst experience I've ever had. Everyone was so fashionable on the street. I almost mistook that I was on the runway. I was wearing a pair of flats! Flats! And I'm so tiny! Arg, so yeah, that was the time I felt like I should change the way I dressed.

我去年在米蘭的時候，第一天到的時候，我覺得我立刻需要一個大改造。而且那是我唯一一天沒什麼打扮，然後那就變成我最糟的經驗了。每個在街上的人都超時尚的。我差點以為我是在參展台上。我那時候正好穿了一雙平底鞋！平底鞋耶！我那麼小隻！哎！所以那就是我覺得我需要立刻改變我打扮方式的時候。

Matt 麥特

Question 37 | 你有沒有曾經在旅行的時候覺得你應該要改變你打扮的方式？

I immediately felt like I needed to change the way I dressed when I arrived in Peru. I'd been very blessed to travel all summer long, following the eternal sunshine. However, in the south hemisphere, it was winter! I had to get my alpaca coat right away.

我一到秘魯就馬上覺得到我要立刻改變我的穿著。我整個夏天都很幸運可以在無止盡的陽光下旅行。但是在南半球的時候，就變成冬天了！我那時候必須要立刻去買駝馬大衣。

When I was traveling in Honduras, I dressed the way I would dress every day here in the U.S. A white tank top and a pair of shorts. However, I started to see guys looking at me in a very weird way. They checked my whole body out unapologetically. I quickly looked around me and found out that no tourists were dressed like me. I quickly went back to the hotel and changed to less revealing dress.

當我在洪都拉斯的時候，我就穿我平常在美國穿得這樣。一件白色背心跟短褲。但是我突然開始發現那裡的男人用很奇怪的眼光看我。他們是一點也不抱歉的看我全身。我立刻看看周遭的人然後發現那裡的觀光客沒有穿得像我這樣。所以我立刻回飯店換一些比較沒有那麼露的衣服。

一問三答 MP3 107

38 Question

In your opinion, what is the best-dressed city?

對你來說，哪一個城市的人最會穿衣服？

I think people in Paris can dress the best. They dress up even when they dress down! It's amazing to see how effortless it is for them to show their styles. And not just women, men, too are really good at dressing up as well. I'm very impressed with the high percentage of people that can dress well in that city!

我覺得巴黎的人最會穿衣服。他們就算沒打扮也像有打扮。看到他們那麼不費力跟輕鬆的展現出他們的風格真的很厲害。而且還不只是女人而已，男人也是很會打扮。我對於他們那裡的人那麼高比例的會穿衣服感到很震撼。

I think people in Hawaii know how to dress the best! Did you know that Aloha shirts are considered formal wear there? Most of their outfits are no more than bikinis, swimming shorts, beachwear, and flip-flops.

The most important part is that it is okay to dress like that, too!

我覺得在夏威夷的人最會穿衣服！你知道夏威夷花襯衫在這裡是正式的穿著嗎？他們大多數的服裝就是比基尼、泳褲、海灘服飾還有夾腳拖鞋。最重要的是他們這樣穿也是可以被接受的！

I think Korean people have a very distinct style, and I find it very cool. They are usually very confident and they have very different styles from the rest of the world. The colors in their outfits are very bold and so are the styles. They are not afraid to show themselves in my opinion!

我覺得韓國人有很獨特的穿衣風格而且我覺得很酷。他們通常都很有自信，而且他們的風格跟其他地方的人也很不一樣。他們服裝的用色都很大膽而且他們的風格也是。我覺得他們真的很不怕展現他們自己。

一問三答 MP3 108

39 Question

What is one specialty food you tried and you would want to go back and eat it again?

你有沒有吃過哪一個名產是你想要再回去吃一次的？

I tried the prosciutto with cantaloupe in Italy. I was a bit skeptical at the beginning because it was basically raw ham with melon, but when I tried it, it was the perfect marriage of the foods. It's savory and sweet, very juicy and simply divine. This appetizer is definitely the embodiment of "Less is more." I tried it in a couple of restaurants here, but it wasn't quite the same.

我在義大利有吃過帕馬火腿（煙薰過很薄的火腿）和哈密瓜。一開始我很懷疑這個生火腿跟香瓜的組合，可是我一吃就發現這個組合真是太完美了。又鹹又甜，而且非常多汁，反正就是很完美。這個開胃菜真的是實踐「少就是多」。我有在這裡的幾家餐廳點這個，可是就是跟在義大利吃到的那個不太一樣。

I would definitely go back to Spain for their Paella. It just has everything I love. Seafood, rice, saffron spices, ...etc. I just love it. I even knew I was going to love it when I saw it. The smell was just impossible to resist. And once I tried it, I knew I was hooked. I would definitely go back again and again for that.

我一定會回去西班牙吃他們的西班牙海鮮燉飯。那燉飯裡面有我所有喜歡吃的東西。海鮮、飯、番紅花香料等等。我超愛的。我一開始光看到那道菜我就知道我會超愛這道菜的。那道菜的味道是無法抵擋的。而且我一吃，我就知道我上癮了。我一定會回去很多次去吃這道菜。

I would want to go back to Australia for their meat pies. I love how the Aussies make their pies savory. There are so many great restaurants that specialized in making meat pies as well, so imagine the competition. You gotta be good enough to sell your meat pie! I always check on the reviews on YELP before I go in any restaurants. Therefore, so far my experiences with meat pies are still really satisfactory.

我會想要回澳洲吃他們的肉派。我很喜歡澳洲人把他們的派做成鹹的！而且那裡也有很多餐廳是專賣肉派的，所以你可以想像那裡的競爭。你一定要夠厲害才可以賣你的肉派！而且我去任何餐廳前都會先用yelp查一下評價，所以目前為止我在那吃過的肉派都很令我滿意！

一問三答 MP3 109

40 Question

What is the scariest thing you tried? How was it?

你吃過最恐怖的是什麼？吃起來怎麼樣？

Michelle 蜜雪兒

Puffer fish sashimi in Japan was the scariest thing I've ever tried. I can literally say that I risked my life trying this dish. Sweat was coming out from my palms when I knew that there was still a very small chance for me to get seriously poisoned eating this dish. Normally, I wouldn't do that, but I just really wanted to challenge myself on this one. So that I can tell you that I've tried it. It wasn't too cheap, but the meat tasted really pure and clean. It was a good dining experience, but it was not worth risking my life. Nevertheless, I'm still glad to say that I've tried it.

我在日本吃的河豚生魚片是至今我吃過最恐怖的東西。我真的可以說我是冒著生命危險吃了這道菜。當我知道還是有很小的機會會嚴重中毒的時候，我的掌心都在冒汗。正常來說我不會想要吃，可是我真的很想挑戰，所以現在我可以跟你說我試過了。它其實沒有很便宜，但是那個肉質真的很純淨和乾淨。那是一個還不錯的美食體驗，可是我是覺得不值得我冒生命危險啦！不過我還是很高興我試過了。

Have you heard of “balut” before? It’s the developing duck embryo people eat in Southeast Asia. Yep, it’s a boiled egg with actual developing duckling inside. The first time I saw it by the street in Vietnam, I thought they just accidentally picked the wrong egg! Little did I know that they chose the ones with the ducklings inside on purpose! I had to try it just for the sake of it. I am still a little freaked out till now. It was scary, but supposedly they are really nutritious and restorative food for women that are pregnant.

你有聽過「鴨仔蛋」嗎？它就是東南亞人會吃的正在發育中的鴨胚胎蛋。對的，就是水煮蛋裡面有一隻正在發育中的真的小鴨子。我第一次在越南的路邊看到的時候還以為他們是不小心選錯蛋了，結果後來才知道他們就是故意要選裡面有小鴨子的！就是看在這麼奇怪的份上，我當時一定要吃一下。我現在還是有點嚇壞了。真的很恐怖，但是據說對懷孕的人是很有營養也是對修復身體很好的。

The scariest thing I have ever tried was the stinky Tofu in Taiwan. It is notorious for its stinkiness, but the crazy part is that the stinkier it is, the better it is according to the locals.The reason why it is stinky is because it’s basically fermented Tofu. Gross, I know, but the locals deep-fried the tofu and served it with Kim chi. I gotta say that it did not taste as scary as it smelled and that I'm glad I gave it a try.

我吃過最恐怖的是台灣的臭豆腐！它就是以它的臭惡名昭彰！但是奇怪的是當地人說越臭越好吃。會這麼臭的原因是因為它是發酵過後的豆腐。很噁心我知道，但是當地人油炸豆腐，然後再放泡菜在上面。我必須說其實它吃起來沒有聞起來那麼可怕，而且我很高興我有試試看。

一問三答 *MP3 110*

41 Question

Are you a mall person? Why? Why not?

你是一個喜歡購物中心的人嗎？為什麼？或為什麼不是？

Michelle 蜜雪兒

Am I a mall person? Excuse me, I can live in a mall. Of course, I am a mall person, and I'm not shameful about it at all. I love everything about shopping in a mall. You get your nails done, you take home beautiful clothes, and you can sit down at the food court to eat or get a cup of gourmet coffee. There is just so much to see and try on. It is a stress-relief process for me really. Don't you just want to get out and shop a little when you are having a bad day? It just makes everything better.

我喜歡購物中心嗎？不好意思，我還可以住在購物中心裡。我當然喜歡購物囉，而且我一點也不害羞。我喜歡購物的每件事。你可以做指甲，帶漂亮的衣服回家，你還可以在美食街吃東西或喝杯高級的咖啡。在購物中心裡有好多東西可以看跟試穿。對我來說其實真的是一個抒壓的方式。你在心情不好的時候不會想要去買點東西嗎？購物讓每件事情都變得很美好。

No, not even a tiny bit. I guess I just don't find material things attractive. Nevertheless, I do have a thing for sporting goods. I guess I don't like shopping, but I do need to get necessities. Yep, that's what I'm trying to say.

一點都不是。物質的東西就真的是一點都不吸引我。不過啦，運動用品店對我來說是我的死穴。我想可能是因為我不喜歡購物，但是我還是得買一些必需品啦。嗯，沒錯，我的意思就是那樣。

Sometimes. I am when there are sales. I don't mind digging out all the goodies even if it means it'll take hours. It's the result that counts. I often find goods that are way under their original prices. It's amazing how much discount you can get sometimes. Who buys with the original prices nowadays?

有的時候是，他們特價的時候我就是。我不介意挖好貨甚至是好幾個小時也沒關係。結果最重要。我常找到很多比原價便宜超多的東西。有的時候看到你拿到多少折扣也是蠻驚人的。現在哪有人用原價買東西啊？

一問三答 *MP3 111*

42 Question

What do you usually shop for when you are traveling?

你旅行的時候通常想要逛街買什麼？

Michelle 蜜雪兒

I like to get things that are made from that place. It just brings back the memories when I see the things I get from those places... Alright...and it's easier for me to remember where I went. It's the true purpose of a souvenir! And I also feel like I can blend in when I'm wearing the stuffs that are made by the local designers there.

我喜歡買是從那個地方製造的東西。當我看到那些東西就會帶我回到在那裡時的回憶…好啦，而且對我來說也比較容易記得我去了哪裡。那就是紀念品真正的意義啊！而且在那裡的時候穿當地設計師做的東西也讓我覺得我比較融入當地！

Like I said, I don't really shop that much at all. However, I like to collect the travel destination magnets when I'm traveling. I always look for a cool one when I'm traveling. I've already had an awesome collection at home. I think I'll need to get a bigger refrigerator next. Hahaha...

就像我剛剛說的，我真的不太喜歡買東西。但是，因為我旅行的時候喜歡收集旅遊景點的磁鐵。我每次旅行的時候都在找一些酷的磁鐵。我在家裡已經有一些很棒的收集。我想我下個要買的東西應該就是一個大一點的冰箱了！哈哈哈…。

I usually shop for local goods that aren't too expensive. I need to get some souvenirs for my boss and coworkers. It's just a nice gesture you know. Foods are usually great to get, or anything that's not too heavy and doesn't take too much room in my luggage really. Handcrafted wares are perfect for example.

我通常喜歡買一些當地的產品，但又不會太貴。因為我通常需要買一些紀念品給我的老闆還有同事。這是一個蠻好表示好意的舉動。食物通常都不錯，或是任何不會太重或是佔我的行李太多空間的東西。例如手工藝品就是很棒的選擇！

一問三答 MP3 112

43 Question

How do you usually decide which restaurants you are going to?
你通常都怎麼決定要去哪一間餐廳的？

There is no reason to eat poorly when you are on vacation. That's why usually before I go anywhere in the world, I make sure the meals are great. Restaurant experience, of course, is a big part of the whole trip. Besides, asking local tour guides directly, I usually just ask the front desk of my hotels for recommendations. They haven't failed me so far. Knock on wood!

你在度假的時候實在沒有理由吃很差。這也就是為什麼通常在我決定要去任何地方之前，我會先確認餐點會是很棒的。在餐廳裡的體驗算是佔了旅行很大一部分。除了直接問我當地的導遊之外，我也會到飯店前櫃台請求提供建議。他們從未讓我失望。老天保佑！

I usually just go with the flow and take a chance. You never know whom you are going to meet and what you might get into. That's why I never make any reservation when I'm going to the restaurants. Most of the time, I meet people and they usually have something in mind. Other times, I just go to any restaurant that I think is interesting. I found many cool little places this way. I might have trouble finding it again, but hey, that's the magical part about it.

我通常就是跟著感覺走耶，然後就冒個險。你永遠不知道你會遇到誰或是會遇到什麼事。這也就是為什麼如果我要去餐廳吃飯的話，我從來都不訂位。大部分的時候，我遇到的人都會有想要去的地方。其他的時候，我就去我覺得蠻有趣的餐廳看看。我都是這樣找到一些很酷的小地方。要我找到去過的餐廳可能有點難，但欸，那也就是它神奇的地方！

Yelp is actually very useful in this case. You will be surprised by how many users it has around the globe. I read the foodie blogger's suggestions and then I Yelp those places. So far, the experiences have been more than satisfactory. I also like to explore APPs, there are a lot of APPs that can tell you where there are some good restaurants people like around your location. The bottom line is that if you do your research and you will get the food that's closer to your expectation.

Yelp 在這個時候就很有用耶！你如果知道全球有多少人在用的話你一定會很驚訝。我會先查美食部落客的建議，然後再用 Yelp 查查看那個地方。目前為止我都很滿意啦。我也會用一些 APP，現在有很多APP 都可以跟你說離你很近的地方大家喜歡的餐廳在哪裡。反正最重要的就是，你一定要做好功課，那你就會吃到跟你預期比較接近的食物啦！

一問三答 MP3 113

44 Question

In your opinion, what makes a restaurant great?

對你而言，一個好的餐廳要有什麼？

Michelle
蜜雪兒

I think obviously what makes a restaurant great is its food. The quality of the food should be over the top and it speaks for all. All those five star restaurants work so hard to make sure the quality of the food is great and they always have innovative dishes. One of my pet peeves is to go to a good restaurant and not be able to get good food there. It's just sad.

我覺得很顯然的一個好餐廳一定要有一很好的食物啊！食物的品質應該要很好，那剩下的就沒話說了。所有五星級的飯店都為了食物的品質而努力，而且他們也通常都會有很多創新的菜肴。我的死穴之一就是去一個好餐廳但是卻吃不到好的食物。就只會讓我覺得很悲哀。

I think what makes a restaurant great is its fun atmosphere. Eating in a restaurant for me is about the whole dining experience. It's not just the food that I'm going for. I'm going to the restaurant for the music, the fun crowd of people, and if the food happens to be great, too, then awesome. But for me it's not the most important thing.

我覺得一個好的餐廳一定要有很好玩的氣氛。我在餐廳吃飯比較在意的是吃飯整體的經驗。我不是只有為了食物而去的。我去是為了那個餐廳的音樂，好玩的人們，然後如果剛好食物也很好吃的話，那就太棒了。但是對我來說，那並不是最重要的事。

I think what makes the restaurant great is its staff. I think if the restaurant staffs care about their food, it makes such a big difference. The service, the food, the place will be great and it's easy to see if the staff care about their own restaurant, too. If the owner can train their employees right, I think it's not hard to have a great restaurant. Better yet, if they have a reasonable price, too, then it'll be an amazing restaurant.

我覺得一個好餐廳一定要有好的員工。如果餐廳的員工在意他們的食物的話，那就會很不一樣。他們的服務、食物，還有整個地方都會很棒因為他們的員工在意他們自己的餐廳。如果餐廳老闆可以好好的訓練員工的話，我想有個好餐廳應該不是難事。更好的是，如果餐廳價格也很好的話，那就會變成一家超級棒的餐廳。

一問三答 MP3 114

45 Question

Do you prefer restaurants that are cheap and cheerful or very fancy?

你比較喜歡便宜又歡樂的餐廳還是高級餐廳？

I prefer restaurants that are fancy. You know how it goes. It's nice to dress up and get all dolled up when you are going to a nice restaurant. Then you don't have to worry about getting food poisoned but just relaxed and enjoy your dinner. And better yet, if you have a handsome date and then the romantic atmosphere will be very important.

我比較喜歡高級餐廳。你知道的。如果要去一間好的餐廳的話，你可以穿得和打扮得很漂亮。然後你也不用擔心會不會食物中毒，可以放鬆的吃飯。更棒的是，如果你有一個很帥的伴的話，那浪漫的氣氛就是很重要的事！

I prefer the cheap and cheerful restaurants so much more! I was once at this restaurant in Hamburg. It wasn't a fancy restaurant, but the food is really good. My friends and I were just having fun and enjoying ourselves. We didn't realize that we stayed past the restaurant closing time. We apologized, but the owner just shrugged and said he was glad to see us having so much fun at his restaurant. It has become our favorite restaurant ever since then.

我比較喜歡去便宜又好玩的地方更多！有一次我在德國漢堡的一間餐廳吃飯。那不是一間很高級的餐廳，但是食物卻非常好吃。我朋友跟我就只是很享受我們的晚餐。我們沒發現我們待到超過關門的時間。我們跟老闆道歉，但他只是聳聳肩跟我們說他很開心看到我們在他的餐廳玩得那麼開心。從那時候開始那裡就是我們最喜歡的餐廳了。

You know, food is food. I don't really feel comfortable spending a lot of money at restaurant. What I care more is if we are full, and if we have fun! I don't know how some restaurant can feel comfortable charging people so much money for a meal and usually tiny meals as well. I guess I just don't get it.

你知道的，食物就是食物。如果我花很多錢在餐廳的食物上的話，我會覺得不自在。我只在意我們有沒有吃飽，還有有沒有玩得盡興！我不知道為什麼很多餐廳可以為了一餐，自在地跟顧客要那麼多錢。我想我就是不懂這個啦。

一問三答 MP3 115

46 Question

What's the best museum you've been to?
你去過最棒的博物館是什麼？

The best one I've been to is Le Louvre in Paris. The museum itself is an art already, not to mention the famous artworks inside. It took me a while to wait till it was my turn to see Mona Lisa. It's beautiful, but I have to say it was smaller than how I had imagined it. However, I think the best way to store beautiful arts is to store them in a beautiful building. They do it right in Paris!

我去過最棒的博物館是在巴黎的羅浮宮。博物館本身就是一個藝術品了，更別提在裡面那些有名的藝術品。我那時候等了蠻久才換我看蒙娜麗莎的微笑。它真的很美，可是我必須說它比我想像的還要小。但是我想儲存美麗藝術品最好的辦法就是把它們放在漂亮的建築物裡。我想它們在巴黎做得很好！

I normally don't go to museums because I think it's a lot of looking around not knowing what they are for me. However, Bishop Museum in Oahu, Hawaii is a really fun museum. It demonstrates how lava is formed and there are a lot of activities and performances at certain times of the day, such as Hula Dance performance. I didn't get bored at that museum and I took a lot of new knowledge with me home. It was a huge museum, but I was thrilled walking around in it.

我通常都不喜歡去博物館，因為我覺得通常都是要走來走去，可是都不知道在看什麼。但是在夏威夷歐胡島的主教博物館是一個很好玩的博物館。它展示了岩漿是怎麼形成的，而且那裡不一樣的時間也都有不一樣的表演，例如草裙舞表演。我在那個博物館裡都不覺得無聊，而且也學了很多。那裡超大的，可是我在裡面十分興奮地走來走去！

I thought Uffizi Gallery was an excellence in museums. It was overwhelming to see all the famous works gathered together in one museum. Michelangelo, Da Vinci, Raphael and more. I took my time walking from room to room and trying to absorb the fact that those were the works that I read from history books in class.

我覺得義大利烏非茲博物館是博物館裡面的翹楚。在一個博物館裡面看到那麼多有名的作品其實蠻震撼的。米開朗基羅、達文西、拉斐爾等等。我在每個展示間裡都慢慢地逛然後盡可能地相信在我眼前都是在歷史課本裡面讀到的那些作品。

一問三答 MP3 116

47 Question

What's the strangest museum you've heard of?

你聽過最奇怪的博物館是什麼？

Michelle 蜜雪兒

I heard there's a Museum of Bad Art at Somerville Massachusetts. That's just so out of the box! Normally, we see amazing or beautiful arts in a museum, but in that museum, they look for bad art which has to be original as well. I'm not too sure about the point of the museum yet. Perhaps you can help me?

我有聽說一間在美國薩莫維爾市的糟糕藝術博物館。那真是太有創意了。通常我們都只會在博物館裡看見很棒或是很美的藝術，但是在他們這間博物館，他們要找的是原創就很糟糕的藝術。我現在還是有點不懂他們的用意。或許你可以告訴我？

The strangest museum I've heard of is the Momofuku Ando Instant Ramen Museumat at Osaka, Japan. The whole museum is decorated with instant noodles, and they also have a section where people can try to make their own instant noodles. That is just so bizarre to me.

我聽過最奇怪的是日本大阪的泡麵發明博物館。整間博物館都是由泡麵所佈置而成的，而且他們也有一區是人們可以來試試看怎麼製作泡麵的。對我來說真的超奇怪的。

The Museum of Broken Relationships in Croatia is by far the strangest museum I've heard of. What do you do with the stuff that belongs to your past relationships? I put them in a box or throw them away, but this museum is looking for those remnants of a broken relationship. It's really strange but I'm with them. I think it's so creative.

在克羅埃西亞有一間失戀博物館是我目前為止聽過最奇怪的博物館。你失戀之後都怎麼處理那些屬於之前戀情的東西啊？我都把它們放到箱子裡或是丟掉，可是這間博物館都在找那些過去戀情遺留下的的東西。那真的很奇怪，但是我蠻喜歡他們的點子的。好有創意。

一問三答 MP3 117

48 Question

If you had lots of money to start your own museum, what would you exhibit in it? And what would you call it?

如果你有很多錢可以開你自己的博物館，你會想要展示什麼？你會叫那間博物館什麼呢？

Michelle 蜜雪兒

It may be a cliché, but I really want to own a Shoe Museum, and I would name it "In Her Shoes". If I had a lot of money already, I'd like to spend it on shoes. Where do I put all those shoes? How about in a museum? It's the most direct way people can appreciate my great taste in shoes.

聽起來可能很陳腔濫調，可是我真的很想要有我自己的鞋子博物館，而且我會叫它「在她的鞋子裡」如果我已經有很多錢了，我想要花在鞋子上。那我要把鞋子放在哪裡咧？博物館聽起來還不錯吧？那是最直接讓大家看到我對鞋子好品味的辦法。

Matt 麥特

I want to open something extraordinary. It's not a tangible thing, but

I think people tend to forget them sometimes. I want to open a "dream" Museum. Dream as in what they want to achieve. I just want to collect many people's dreams and put them together to remind people not to forget them. I would name it: "Museum of the Thing You Call Your Dream".

我想要開一間特別的。那不是具體的東西，可是我們大家常常忘記它。我想要開「夢」的博物館。我是說你想達成的夢想的夢。我想要收集大家的夢想，然後把它們放在一起來提醒大家別忘了他們的夢想。我會叫他：「夢想這個東西博物館」。

If I had a lot of money, I would like to open a Book Museum. There is so much work included to produce a book. A book is an identity, a voice or message the author is trying to tell the world. Everything from the book cover design to the content has been pondered upon thousands of times. The best way is to collect some of the best ones and put them together. It would be called something like "behind the pages".

如果我有很多錢的話我會想要開一間書的博物館。要製造一本書要花好多工夫。一本書是一個身份，一個聲音或是一個作者要傳達給世界的訊息。從封面設計到內容的製作都是被想過好多次的結果。我覺得最好就是搜集很多最好的書，然後把它們放在一起。我可能會叫他「在書的每一頁之後」之類的。

一問三答 MP3 118

49 Question

What famous architecture would you like to visit one day?

你有天有想要去哪個有名的建築物嗎？

Michelle 蜜雪兒

I really want to see Taj Mahah in Agra, India one day! It's a mausoleum of a Persian princess who was the favorite wife of the emperor at the time. After she passed away, the emperor was so sad, and decided to build this for her. She still died like a princess. I really want to be there and learn about their love story after all this time. How I wish someone would build a mausoleum for me when I die.

我真的很想要去在印度阿格拉的泰姬馬哈陵！那是一個當時皇帝最喜歡的妻子，一個波斯公主的陵墓。在她去世之後，皇帝就十分的傷心，並且決定要為她打造這個陵墓。她就算死也是很公主的。在過了這麼久以後，我也真的很想要去那裡了解他們的愛情故事。我真希望我死的時候也有人幫我蓋一個陵墓。

Matt 麥特

I really want to visit The Great Pyramids of Giza in Egypt. It's on my ultimate bucket list. I love everything about Pyramids, and there are so many movies with the theme of the pyramids. I still cannot believe such structures were built by men. I just want to be there and witness this wonder and mystery.

我真的很想要去埃及的基沙大金字塔。那一直都是在我的終極死前要完成的事項清單中。我很喜歡所有關於金字塔的事，而且也有那麼多部電影都是以金字塔為主題。我還是無法想像這個建築物是人造的。我只想要去那裡目睹這個奇景還有謎。

I haven't had a chance to visit the Great Wall yet, but I really want to visit. They built the wall to keep the enemies from coming into their territory and can you imagine the work they were doing to build the Great Wall? It's 21, 196 km long! And it's from such a long time ago! I really don't know how they made it happen with so little technology back then!

我還沒有機會去過長城，可是我真的很想去。他們當年建造這個牆是為了要避免敵人入侵他們的領土，而且你可以想像他們那時候要花多少功夫嗎？這個長城有兩萬一千一百九十六公里長耶！而且還是從那麼久以前造的！我實在是不知道他們那時候沒什麼科技，怎麼可以建造出這個！

一問三答 MP3 119

50 Question

What is the most amazing building you have ever seen?

你看過最棒的建築是什麼？

The most amazing building I have ever seen is the famous Sagrada Familia built by Gaudi. It's one thing to see it from the picture, but it' another when you see it in person. I thought to myself Gaudi must have lost it. The building is beyond creativity. It's not like anything I've seen before.

我看過最棒的建築是鼎鼎有名的由高第建造的聖家堂。從照片看是一回事，但是真正看到又是另外一回事。我那時候在想說高第一定瘋了。這個建築物已經超越創意了。我從來沒有看到任何像這樣的建築。

By far I have to say Machu Picchu is the most amazing building I've ever seen, especially with the location, too! It's just amazing to be able to live all the way up in the mountain and so secluded, too. The irrigation system there is pretty cool, too. I wonder if there are more

Machu Picchu deeper in the mountain. I wouldn't mind living there at all.

我目前為止是覺得馬丘比丘是我看過最棒的建築，尤其是那個地點！真的很棒他們可以住在深山裡，而且還那麼的隱密。那裡的灌溉系統也很酷。我在想不知道在更深山裡有沒有更多的馬丘比丘。我一點都不介意住在那裡。

I was really impressed with the Lotus Temple in India. The whole building is just extremely peaceful. The shape of the temple is a lotus, and it is all white and you are required to take your shoes off before you enter. They welcome people with every religion to come in and pray at the same space. I really feel at peace in that space.

我對印度的蓮花廟印象很深刻。整個建築都十分的平和。它的外型就是一個蓮花，而且它也是全白的。你要進去廟裡之前要把鞋子脫掉。他們歡迎所有宗教信仰在同一個空間一起來禱告。我在那個空間裡真的覺得很安寧。

一問三答 MP3 120

51 Question

What city's architecture has impressed you the most?

你覺得哪一個城市的建築是最令你印象深刻的？

Barcelona impressed me the most. Besides the Sagrada Familia, there are Gaudi's works spread around the city, and I have to say that I'm impressed with them all. It's like your fantasy come true or your drawing come alive. He has more imagination and creativity than anyone I know. Many great architecture just dots around the city. I love Barcelona.

巴塞隆納最讓我印象深刻。除了聖家堂之外，高第的作品整個城市裡到處都是。我必須說我真的對他們全部都很印象深刻。那就像是你的幻想成真，或是你的圖畫活了起來。他比我知道的任何人都還要有想像力和創意。有很多的建築到處在城中分佈。我愛巴塞隆納。

I am gonna go with Athens. I always have a thing for Greek

Mythology. That was my favorite class in college, too. There are so many pantheons in Athens, and it is such an old town. I just find those buildings fascinating and I mean, that was where the Greek God and Goddess lived! !

我選雅典好了！我一直很喜歡希臘神話。那也是我在大學的時候最喜歡的一堂課。在雅典有好多的神殿，而且這個城市也十分的古老。我覺得這整個城市都很吸引人，我是說這是希臘神和女神住的地方耶！

I think the architecture in Istanbul is pretty impressive. There are a lot of magnificent mosques and colorful coffee shops around every corner. The best thing is that usually the best ones are not too far away from each other. I really enjoyed my day walking trips there. It's very exotic and the architecture definitely adds a lot to the city.

我覺得在伊斯坦堡的建築還蠻令人印象深刻的。那裡有很多雄偉的清真寺，附近還有很多色彩繽紛的咖啡店。最棒的是通常他們最棒的建築都離彼此不遠。我在那裡的時候真的很享受我白天的走路遊覽。非常有異國風味而且那裡的建築真的為那個城市加分了不少。

一問三答 MP3 121

52 Question

Have you been to any bike friendly countries? How was it?

你有去過哪些騎腳踏車很方便的國家嗎？好玩嗎？

Michelle
蜜雪兒

Yes, I was in Copenhagen, Denmark. The city really surprised me with how bike friendly it was. There are bike lanes throughout the city. I never had to share the road with other motor vehicles. I felt pretty safe biking around the city. I'm not the strongest in biking, but I have to say it was relatively easy to bike around in Copenhagen. I mean I wasn't whining or pouting at all!

有啊，我去了丹麥的哥本哈根。我真的還蠻驚訝那個城市竟然騎腳踏車那麼方便。整個城市裡都有自行車道。我從頭到尾都不用跟其他的車擠同一個車道。我那時候覺得在那個城市裡騎自行車是還蠻安全的。我騎腳踏車沒有很強，可是我得說在那城市騎車還蠻容易的。我都沒抱怨還是嘛嘴欸。

Matt
麥特

Yes, I've been to Amsterdam in the Netherlands. It was really amazing to see the biking population there. It's very common that everyone rides bikes, and rarely do people own cars. The parking lots for the bikes are jaw dropping. It was immense. I literally stood there and wowed for a minute. There are traffic lights for the bikes, bike lanes, all the basics and beyond. I thought it was intriguing to see people all dressed up for work on a bike. They bike with style for sure.

我有去荷蘭的阿姆斯特丹。在那裡騎腳踏車的人口真的很驚人。在那裡大家騎腳踏車是很正常的事，反而比較少人開車。腳踏車的停車場也很令人掉下巴。超大的。我那時候真的是就站在那裡驚呼了一分鐘。那裡有腳踏車紅綠燈、自行車道，所有基本的還有其他的都有。而且我也覺得看著腳踏車上的人們打扮好去上班很有趣。他們真的是騎腳踏車也要很有風格。

I was in Berlin and my Airbnb host left me a bike to explore the city. I thought that was very nice of him, so I took the bike out and biked around the city. There were a lot of people biking around the city, and it was a really good way to get to know the city. Berlin struck me as a top student in class, but he also dresses very nicely and very chic. What was my point...I just lost my train of thought.

我在柏林的時候，我 Airbnb 的主人留了一輛腳踏車給我去探索那個城市。我那時候覺得他人很好，於是我就帶了腳踏車出去蹓躂。那裡也有很多人在騎腳踏車，而且我覺得那真的是一個認識那個城市的好方式。柏林讓我覺得他好像是一個班上頂尖的學生，但是又很會打扮很時髦。我想說的是什麼…我的思路亂掉了啦。

一問三答 MP3 122

53 Question Do you enjoy touring by bike? Why? Why not?
你喜歡用腳踏車觀光嗎？為什麼或是為什麼不喜歡？

Michelle 蜜雪兒

I like it, but it's not my top choice. There are some advantages of touring by bike. It's really easy to park them, and the breeze is nice. However, on the other hand, if it's a hot day, then it'll ruin your trip. I'll just ride to the nearest coffee shop and call it a day.

我喜歡，可是那不是我最喜歡的選項。用腳踏車觀光有很多好處。很好停車，然後微風也很舒服。但是，另外一方面來說，如果今天很熱的話，那就會毀了你的旅程。我應該會騎到最近的咖啡店，然後就結束今天的行程。

Matt 麥特

I love touring by bike if I'm given the choice. You can go wherever you go without worrying too much about traffic jams. You don't hide yourself on the bike. On the contrary, you're exposed to the place. You have to say hi to people and you have to listen, and smell the place. I understand it could go both good and bad in that sense, but for me I'm willing to take the risks.

如果可以的話我非常喜歡用腳踏車觀光。你可以去任何地方然後也不用太擔心塞車，而且你在腳踏車上面沒辦法躲起來。相反的，你是暴露在那個地方的。你遇到認識的人的時候一定要打招呼，你也一定要聽或是聞這個地方。我知道那樣可能會很好或是很不好。但是我會想要冒那個險，用這種方式體驗這個城市。

Yes, I do actually. It's cheap and you can see a lot when you are on a bike, too! Of course I can't go as far as when I'm in the car, but I think a bike will do. It's just a very organic way to tour around the place, and really slow down to see what is around you. Have you ever ridden racing bikes, mountain bikes, BMX bikes or other recreational bikes?

嗯，我真的很喜歡。因為它是很便宜的方式，而且在腳踏車上你也可以看到很多。我當然是不會像在開車的時候一樣去那麼遠，但是我想腳踏車就夠了啦。那是一種很有機的觀光方式，而且同時間也可以慢下來並且看看在你身邊的事物。你有騎過公路車、登山車、BMX 整車或是其它休閒腳踏車嗎？

一問三答 MP3 123

54 Question

What type of accommodation do you usually stay in when you travel? Why?

你旅行的時候通常都比較喜歡哪一種住宿方式？為什麼？

Michelle 蜜雪兒

I usually just go with the hotels. It's easy and safe, and really, do you really want to clean up your mess before you leave when you are on vacation? Pay a little bit extra to get the peace of mind. I think it's worth it.

我通常都會選擇住飯店。又簡單又安全，而且說真的，你真的想要在度假時離開前還要打掃嗎？付多一點換來一點心安，我是覺得很值得啦。

Matt 麥特

Couchsurfing for sure. I know how some people would have concerns about the safety of Couchsurfing, but the website has so many safety measures in play. It's really not bad at all. I love Couchsurfing because that's where the magic of traveling happens. You get to mingle with your local host and possibly their friends. It, in a way, is forcing you to make friends, and I like that idea.

我一定是選沙發衝浪。我知道有些人會對沙發衝浪有安全的考量，但是其實它網站上有做了許多安全的措施。其實沒那麼糟。我很愛沙發衝浪，因為那就是旅行神奇的地方。你可以跟當地的主人或是主人的朋友交流。而且其實沙發衝浪有一點強迫你去交朋友，我真的很喜歡那樣。

I like to use Airbnb. It's usually good deal if you play it right. And different from Couchsurfing, you don't always see your host. Most of the time they just give you a separate room or even the whole place to yourself. I like the price and I also want my privacy.

我喜歡用 Airbnb. 其實你用對戰術的話，它通常都是很便宜的。而且跟沙發衝浪不同的是，你不一定會見到你的住宿主人。大部分時候他們都會給你另外一間房間，或甚至是留整個地方給你。我喜歡它的價錢，也想要我自己的隱私。

一問三答 MP3 124

55 Question

Do you have any interesting stories at the accommodation when you were traveling?

你有沒有一些旅行的時候關於住宿有趣的故事？

Michelle
蜜雪兒

I was staying at the Four Seasons Hotel in Miami and found out that a local celebrity and his family were staying next to my room. I didn't really know him since I didn't really watch TV that much, but from what the housekeepers told me, he was really popular, but he was a very difficult customer.

我在邁阿密的時候住在四季酒店，然後發現隔壁住的是當地的名人和他的家人。我不認識他因為我沒什麼在看電視，但飯店的管家跟我說，他在當地很受歡迎，但他真是一個大奧客。

Matt
麥特

Once I was on a hiking trip in Europe. I didn't have Internet to book my hostel, so I could only go to the hostel after I finished the hike that day. It was after sunset, and the only hostel in the town was all booked out. They only had one private room available, but it would cost me 60 dollars. I didn't have that much budget, so sadly I had to leave. However, miraculously, the owner of the hostel asked me if I could help him fold the sheets, and if I helped him, I could get the room for free. So I did it happily, and miraculously earned my private room and a great night sleep for free.

有一次我去歐洲健行旅行。我身上沒有網路可以訂青年旅社，所以我只好健行完再去青年旅社訂房間。那時候已經是日落，而且那間鎮上唯一的一間青年旅社房間也完全被訂完了。他們只剩下一間單人房，但是一間要價六十元美金。我沒有那麼多預算，所以只好難過的要離開。但神奇的是，青年旅社的主人突然問我可不可以幫他折床單，他說如果我可以幫他的話，我就可以免費住在那個房間。所以我就很高興地幫他折床單，而且奇蹟似地賺到我的單人房，還有一覺好眠。

So there are times when you cannot hide from your host from Airbnb. This is one of the examples. I went to the meeting place to get my room key from my host in India. However, she insisted that I should join her for their family reunion that evening. The next thing I knew, I was sitting in the middle of a big Indian family and taking family photographs.

有時候你沒辦法躲過你的 Airbnb 住宿主人。這就是其中的一個例子。我在印度去了約好見面的地方跟住宿主人拿鑰匙。但是，她堅持要我加入她們家晚上的家族聚會。我反應過來的時候，我就坐在一個印度大家族的中間，跟她們拍家族合照。

一問三答 MP3 125

56 Question

What do you care the most about your accommodation?

你對住宿最重視的是什麼？

Michelle 蜜雪兒

Service! Duh! It is fair to demand great service when you pay quite a bit of money. I'm not trying to be difficult, but the whole point of traveling is that you want to enjoy your vacation. Otherwise, I can just stay home. Do you see where I'm coming from?

當然是服務囉！當你花那麼多錢的時候，我覺得要求好的服務是很公平的。我不是想當奧客，但是旅行的目的不就是要享受嗎？不然我就待在家就好啦。你懂我的邏輯嗎？

Matt 麥特

I always go with the host that can offer the most local experiences. Isn't it the whole point of traveling? To see other culture and what people do in difference places? Since I always Couchsurf, local experiences would be the things I am constantly looking for.

我都是選有提供當地體驗的住宿主人。那就是旅行的重點不是嗎？去看其他的文化還有人們在不一樣的地方做的事情。因為我是沙發客，所以有沒有當地體驗就是我找住宿的重點。

As much as I like to budget myself, I really care about how clean a place is. It doesn't have to be spotless, but it has to be at least clean and livable. I don't want to get bitten by the "real" travel bug home.

就算我很小心花錢，我真的很重視一個地方乾不乾淨。不用到一塵不染，可是至少要整潔和宜居。我不想要被「真的」旅遊蟲子咬到。

一問三答 MP3 126

57 Question

What forms of transportation do you usually use when you are traveling? Why?
你在旅行的時候通常會用什麼交通工具？為什麼？

Michelle 蜜雪兒

I usually go with the driver guide service. I really don't feel like handling the stress of looking for directions or getting lost when I'm traveling. I just want to use time in the most efficient way. If someone can drive for me and take me to the spots I'm interested in with local knowledge, it's like I have a friend in that country. In a way, I hire a local friend for my vacation.

我通常會選擇司機兼導遊的服務。我真的很不想要在旅行的時候還要煩惱找路，或是迷路。我只是想要有效率地利用時間。如果有人可以幫我開車，還可以帶我到我有興趣的地方去玩，那就好像是我在那個國家有一個當地的朋友一樣。其實就好像是我為了我的假期僱用了一個當地的朋友啦。

Matt 麥特

I usually hitchhike when I'm traveling. You will be amazed at how many kind people there are in the world. Sometimes it only takes me 5 minutes to get a ride, but sometimes it takes a couple of hours. It was hard for me to hitchhike at the beginning because I couldn't handle the rejection, but it's just silly thinking back.

我在旅行的時候通常喜歡搭便車。你會很驚訝世界上有多少好人。有的時候只會花五分鐘，可是有的時候要等好幾個小時。一開始的時候其實搭便車對我來說很難，因為我不喜歡被拒絕的感覺，但是現在回想過去我真的是很傻。

Becca
貝卡

It really depends on where I go. There are a lot of places that have metro systems. It's cheap and it's quick. Local people use it, too. If I need to go somewhere remote, I'll go with Uber. It's a new thing though, it's pretty much an app you can request rides from wherever you are. It's usually cheaper than a taxi, so there you go!

真的要看我是去哪裡。其實很多地方都有地鐵。它又便宜又快。當地人也會使用它。如果我要去很遙遠的地方的話，我就會用 Uber。不過那個還蠻新的。其實它就是一個 APP 你可以在你所在的地方叫車。而且通常他還比計程車便宜，當然是選他囉！

一問三答 MP3 127

58 Question

What are some local transportation you took and thought they were cool?

你有沒有坐過什麼當地的交通工具，然後覺得他們很酷的？

Michelle 蜜雪兒

I was in Venice and of course I had to try the Gondola ride, but I went with the slightly fancier one. My gondola offered a private tour and it came with the singers and the musicians. It was really romantic, but I didn't really have a date, so it was actually a little bit awkward. Well, it was really cool though.

我在威尼斯的時候當然要試試看貢多拉，但是我是選了比一般高級一點點的。我的貢多拉有私人導覽，而且船上還有歌手和樂手。真的很浪漫但是我那個時候沒有伴啦，所以其實有點尷尬。不過還是蠻酷的就是了。

Matt 麥特

I was taking the Tuk Tuk in Vietnam and it wasn't really the safest ride I took. I felt like the vehicle was about to break at any time. Strange enough, I enjoyed the ride as my driver was weaving through the traffic in the middle of Ho Chi Minh City. It was a pretty unique experience.

我在越南的時候有坐嘟嘟車，它真的不是我坐過算很安全的。我覺得那車好像隨時都會垮掉一樣。很奇怪的是，我的司機在胡志明市中穿梭在車陣之間時，我其實是還蠻喜歡的。那是一個蠻獨特的體驗。

I was in Florida riding the Segway while I was touring around. I felt like a really lazy person from the future, but it was really awesome. It was easy to control and it gets me to where I need to go without too much effort...Oh my god, I sound like a really lazy person from the future...

我在佛羅里達州的時候有用賽格威（電動代步車）到處遊覽。我那時候覺得我真的很像是從未來來的很懶惰的人，但是那真的很棒耶！它很簡單控制而且也很輕鬆就帶我到我需要去的地方…我的天啊，我聽起來好像是從未來來的很懶惰的人。

一問三答 MP3 128

59 Question

Do you have any bad experience about transportation when you are traveling?
你旅行的時候有沒有遇過什麼關於交通工具不好的經驗？

Michelle
蜜雪兒

It wasn't bad, but it caught me by surprise. When I was in Bangkok, my friends and I wanted to go to this local bar far away, so naturally we wanted to take a taxi. It should be a great thing for the taxi driver, right? If we want to go somewhere far from where we got picked up. But no, no taxi drivers would take us because it was too far. We ended up going to a different bar.

是沒有很糟，可是有出乎我的意料之外。我在曼谷的時候，我的朋友和我想要去一個蠻遠的當地酒吧，所以很自然的我們想要搭計程車。如果我們要去離我們上車很遠的地方，對計程車司機應該是很好不是嗎？但是不是，因為太遠了的關係，沒有計程車司機要帶我們去。我們最後只好換去一個不一樣的酒吧。

Matt
麥特

I was going to Alabama for a music festival, but I landed in Atlanta.

I decided to go with Greyhound Bus, which turned out to be a total disaster. The bus never came and I had to catch a different bus to the Greyhound central station. Not only that, the bathroom on the bus was beyond horrible. I don't think I would take the bus again.

我要去阿拉巴馬州參加音樂節，可是我在亞特蘭大下飛機。我那時候決定要做灰狗巴士，結果後來變成一個大災難。那車沒來，所以我要做另外一輛公車到灰狗巴士的總站。不止那樣而已，車上的廁所恐怖的不得了。我想我應該不會再坐他們的公車。

When my friends and I were looking for a taxi to go to our hostel in Vietnam, we tried to ask the taxi drivers if they were running by the meter (recommended by our friends), or we wouldn't take the taxi. No taxi driver would take us until this one guy took us. However, we soon discovered that the meter was broken. We had to ask him to pull over and he got really mad. Luckily there were people around where he stopped the car. That was pretty scary.

我跟我朋友要搭計程車到我們的青年旅社的時候，我們問了那裡的司機他們是不是照里程表算錢（我們的朋友建議的），不然的話，我們就不坐他們的車。沒有人要載我們，後來有一個司機說好。但是我們上車之後很快就發現他的里程表是壞掉的。我們叫他停在路邊，他超級生氣的。幸好他停車的地方有很多人。不過那真的蠻恐怖的。

一問三答 MP3 129

60 Question

Have you ever encountered any emergency during your trip? What happened?

你有曾經在旅行的時候遇到什麼緊急事件嗎？發生了什麼事？

Once when I was traveling to the Caribbean, it took me two days to get there and seven days for my bags to arrive! You can only imagine my dismay. I was utterly destroyed inside. I had bought and matched up all my outfits for my Caribbean trip before I left. Also, all my toiletry and skincare products were all in the luggage. I had to go shopping all over again for the first two days. I didn't mind doing the shopping, but you know how it is with skincare products. There are only certain brands that are perfect for you. It was just depressing thinking about it again.

有一次我到加勒比海旅行，花了我兩天的時間才飛到目的地，但是我的行李七天才到！你可以想像我有多沮喪。我內心完全崩潰。在我出發到加勒比海之前，我已經買好了衣服，也都搭配好每天要穿的了。而且，我的盥洗用品和保養品也都在行李裡。我前兩天都要到處去逛街。逛街我是不介意，可是你知道保養品。他們就是只有某些牌子是完全適合你的。我現在想到就又開始沮喪了。

Question 60 | 你有曾經在旅行的時候遇到什麼緊急事件嗎？發生了什麼事？

I was food poisoned when I was in Cusco. It was bad because I was traveling by myself, and I couldn't do anything besides puking and having diarrhea for the first few days. It was scary because I was too weak to go seek any sort of help. I was just sleeping, woke up to puke and then passed out again. Luckily all the bacteria must have eventually got out of my system, but it was just a bad experience.

我在庫斯科的時候食物中毒。那時候很慘因為我只有一個人在旅行，而且我前幾天除了吐和拉肚子之外完全無法做其他事。那時候很可怕因為我虛弱到完全無法去求救。我就只有睡覺，醒來去吐，然後又昏睡過去。好險最後細菌總算完全脫離我的身體，但那還是一個很糟的經驗。

My friends and I rented a car and we parked it with all the other cars by the road and we went hiking. After we were done hiking, our car was broken into. The windows were broken and our bags were stolen. I hid my wallet in the car and the thieves found it, so I had to cancel all my credit cards, but luckily I didn't have much cash in the wallet. We reported the incident and took the car back to the rental company to switch for a new one since we had purchased the insurance at the beginning.

我朋友跟我租了一台車，我們停在路邊其他車旁，然後我們就去爬山了。我們回來的時候，發現有人打破我們的車子。窗戶都破了，而我們的包包都被偷了。我把我的皮夾藏在車子裡，但是小偷找到了，所以我要掛失一堆信用卡，但是好險我皮夾裡沒有很多現金。我們報了警之後因為一開始有買保險，所以就把車帶回租車的地方換了一輛新的。

一問三答 MP3 130

61 Question

Do you do anything as a precaution to prevent emergencies for your trips?

你有做什麼事來預防旅行的時候緊急事件發生嗎？

Michelle 蜜雪兒

I started to pack one third of my clothes, mini toiletry and skincare products into my carryon bags and the rest in the luggage ever since that horrible incident happened in the Caribbean. Oh, and it's also a good idea to put your money in different places or bags. If you lose one, at least you still have some in other bags. Yeah, they didn't call me a travel expert for no reason.

我自從上次在加勒比海發生那件恐怖的事後，我就開始放三分之一的衣服，迷你的盥洗用品還有保養品在隨身行李裡，然後剩下的再放在托寄行李裡。喔，還有就是要把你的錢放在不一樣的地方，這樣一來，如果你丟掉一筆的話，至少你在其他地方還有錢。沒錯，他們不是平白無故叫我旅遊專家的。

I make extra copies of my passport and visas and put them in different places just in case I lose them. Losing your passport can be a pain in the butt when you are traveling, and unfortunately it happens quite often.

我有多影印了幾份護照和簽證，然後再把它們放在不一樣的包包裡以防我弄丟了護照。在旅行的時候弄丟護照真的超煩的，而且很不幸的是那還很常發生。

I always carry hand sanitizers and avoid eating foods on the street. I took necessary and unnecessary vaccines, stomach medicines, pepper spray, and oh a fake wedding ring!!

我都會隨身攜帶乾洗手液還有不吃路邊的食物。我也會打必要跟不必要的疫苗，帶胃藥、防狼噴霧器，噢對了！還有一個假的結婚戒指！

附錄：額外話題補充

新聞三｜為了救小孩殺了大猩猩 Kill the gorilla to save the kid

美國有個小孩和媽媽逛動物園時，不小心掉進了大猩猩的柵欄裡。大猩猩將小孩從護城河中抓出來，抱在懷裡。因為麻醉針可能會讓大猩猩獸性大發而傷害小孩，為了救出小孩，園方決定槍殺大猩猩。可是大猩猩何其無辜。

新聞四｜新加坡的再生水 New water

新加坡地密人稠，水資源都要向鄰近的馬來西亞購買。為了減少對馬來西亞的依賴，新加坡也不斷研發再生水資源的能力，除了海水淡化還有雨水蒐集之外，新水（New water）則是由汙水淨化而再生成飲用水，可是想到要把汙水喝下肚，心裡真是有點掙扎。

湖泊三｜日月潭 Sun-Moon Lake

去年夏天爸爸決定帶爺爺奶奶出去走一走，所以我們決定到南投的日月潭來個家族旅行。我們的飯店房間可以看到湖景，傍晚的時候湖面上升起濃濃的霧氣，感覺好像置身仙境。隔天早上我們搭船去環湖，經過導遊的解說才知道原來日月潭一邊是日潭，一邊叫月潭，所以才有「日月潭」之稱。

湖泊四｜大學池 University lake

幾個月前，我跟我男朋友去溪頭玩，溪頭有一座有名的湖叫做大學池。大學池上有一座竹子搭的橋叫情人橋，跟男朋友去更是要去走一下。大學池被濃濃的樹林圍住，湖面的反射時而藍、時而綠實在很特別。我最喜歡太陽光透過樹梢映在湖面的感覺。

電器三｜冰箱 Refrigerator

如果沒有冰箱我真的不知道該如何保存食物，尤其是像肉品、鮮奶這種容易腐敗的東西。剩菜、廚餘也必須要丟棄，但是這樣會造成很多的浪費。誰有空天天到市場買菜煮三餐，都不用上班了嗎?冰箱真的是個很棒的發明，而且是每個人都會需要的產品。

電器四｜吸塵器 Vacuum

在吸塵器發明之前，打掃地毯真的是個噩夢！只能用掃的或是拿到室外用特別的地毯刷子，一邊打、一邊刷。清潔效果非常有限，而且塵蹣和細菌根本都清除不掉，衛生上有很大的疑慮。吸塵器真的是造福人群的發明，不然那些對塵蹣過敏的人該怎麼辦呢？

決定三｜買房子 Buying a house

畢業後工作也五、六年了，存了一筆小錢，打算拿來當頭期款買房子。雖然不太夠，可是有爸媽贊助一些也還可以。但是一想到從此之後房貸要背二、三十年，以後也沒有閒錢出國去玩，我還是決定再緩一緩。畢竟我現在也還住家裡，不需要房子。

決定四｜投資理財 Investment

我看朋友投資股市還做得不錯，常常都有賺錢。我也在想是不是要拿點錢出來投資，可是我又不懂股票市場，萬一賠光了我又要從頭開始，不如請我朋友操盤，給她賺點傭金。是有點風險可是我目前還有小賺一點。我覺得有時候就是要放手一搏。

音樂三｜雷鬼音樂 Reggae

我喜歡聽雷鬼音樂因為我不知不覺地就會融入音樂跟著搖擺。尤其是工作壓力大到想去度假的時候。我總是想像著手上拿了杯調酒，靠在海灘上的露天酒吧旁邊，望著藍天碧海，還有沙灘上滿滿的比基尼辣妹，頓時心情好很多。

音樂四｜爵士樂 Jazz

幾年前到紐約找高中同學，他帶我到爵士樂酒吧聽歌。我從此之後就愛上爵士樂那種時而輕快又時而浪漫的節奏。爵士酒吧的氣氛很好，通常並不太大，聽眾跟樂團的距離很近，你可以清楚地感受到演奏者的情緒，很有震撼力。

音樂五｜英文經典情歌 English classic love songs

我從小就喜歡聽英文經典情歌，一開始是因為英文情歌很受歡迎，到處都聽得到，也因為常聽到，所以非常想學會歌詞跟著唱。我買了很多 CD，常常一邊聽一邊看著歌詞學唱，唱多了也開始了解歌詞的意義，因此我還學了不少片語呢！

廣告三｜蠻牛廣告 Taiwanese Red bull

一個很瘦小的老公不斷地為了討好肥老婆而盡力去達成她的要求，一下要煮飯，一下要上班、一下要接小孩，還要幫老婆全身按摩，最後在他上氣不接下氣喘息的時候，背景聲音問他，你累了嗎？他喝了提神飲料之後，立刻精神百倍。

廣告四｜報紙的贈品廣告 Newspaper

一個上班族正要準備早餐，把吐司放進烤麵包機，打開瓦斯爐準備煎個蛋，低下頭去看吐司烤好了沒有，沒想到吐司正好烤好跳起來打到他的眼睛，他不自主地轉身想扶住流理台，沒想到卻是把手放到燒熱的鍋子上，此時出現訂報紙就送急救包的標語。

經驗三｜請人讓座給孕婦 Priority seat

我高中時候需要坐公車上、下課，有一次剛好有位孕婦上車，她手上還提著不少東西，車上人很多，前排位子的人睡著了，我趕緊叫醒他，請他讓座給孕婦。雖然不是我直接讓位給孕婦，但是我覺得我也是做了件好事，她很感謝我。

經驗四｜撿到手機歸還 Return the cellphone

有一次在提款機旁邊撿到一隻手機，我並沒有看到有人在我前面剛領完錢，所以我猜他可能剛走。我也有事不能在原地等，所以我拿他的手機查一下他通訊錄，他有存家裡的電話，我就打過去跟她家人說我撿到他的手機，並留下我的電話跟她約時間請她把手機拿回去。

書籍三｜印度廚房 World kitchen - Indian published by Murdoch books

我很喜歡吃印度菜，可是在台灣印度餐廳並不普遍，而且價格也高，我決定買食譜自己做做看。書裡面除了食譜之外，還有教很多做印度烤餅的技法及秘訣。從中我也認識到很多我們不熟悉的香料種類以及如何應用香料。我試過幾次都蠻成功的。

書籍四｜行銷妙招 Sales psychology by Fong Sheng Lee

我本身是做業務的，所以跟客戶的溝通接洽很重要，我從這本書中學到很多話術還有推敲客戶心思的技巧。也發現我以前的方式不太有效率，因為我沒有找對方法。作者用平易近人的白話方式來寫作，我覺得很容易閱讀，收穫很大。

國家圖書館出版品預行編目(CIP)資料

雅思口說聖經 / Amanda Chou著-- 初版. --
新北市：倍斯特出版事業有限公司, 2021.
08 面；公分. --（考用英語系列；32）
ISBN 978-986-06095-3-0（平裝附光碟）
1.國際英語語文測試系統　2.考試指南

805.189　　110008183

考用英語系列 032

雅思口說聖經（附英式發音MP3）

初　　版　2021年 8月
定　　價　新台幣460元

作　　者　Amanda Chou
出　　版　倍斯特出版事業有限公司
發 行 人　周瑞德
電　　話　886-2-8245-6905
傳　　真　886-2-2245-6398
地　　址　23558 新北市中和區立業路83巷7號4樓
E-mail　best.books.service@gmail.com
官　　網　www.bestbookstw.com
總 編 輯　齊心瑀
特約編輯　陳韋佑
封面構成　高鍾琪
內頁構成　菩薩蠻數位文化有限公司
印　　製　大亞彩色印刷製版股份有限公司

港澳地區總經銷　泛華發行代理有限公司
地　　址　香港新界將軍澳工業邨駿昌街7號2樓
電　　話　852-2798-2323
傳　　真　852-3181-3973

版權所有・翻印必究